THE COURT OF DREAMS

A.J. NORA

Lion Briar Books
INDEPENDENT PUBLISHING

LION BRIAR BOOKS LLC

To request permission, contact the publisher at aj@ajnorabooks.com

Paperback: 978-1-967056-01-9

Ebook: 978-1-967056-00-2

First paperback edition July 2025

Edited by: Atwater Group

Cover Art by: Getcovers

Lion Briar Books

ajnorabooks.com

AUTHOR'S NOTE

This is a closed-door portal fantasy with romance. If you'd like content warnings, please head to my website (https://ajnorabooks.com/content-warnings-for-kingdoms-of-kaelums/ to get the list.)

I believe in representation, and I will always include queer people in my stories because we exist and deserve to see ourselves in the novels we read.

Thank you for supporting an indie author. I hope you enjoy! <3

If you'd like to join my newsletter list, you can do so at https://ajnorabooks.com/newsletter to stay up to date on upcoming books and other exciting news!

For the aspecs like me, who hate having to skim sex scenes all the damn time, but still love fantasy romance.

SILVIS
THE SOMNIUM SEA
DREAMER RIVER
SINK FALLS
KAESY
KHENT
DAES RIVER
SHEEPSGROVE FOREST
SILVER MOUNTAINS
THE ABYSSAL BAY
HOLLOW DESERT
UVIEL
THE CAPITAL
CAINE
SEAI
MAJESTY MARSH
Noord

PRONUNCIATION GUIDE

Silvis: SIL-vis

Brynia:BRI-nee- yah

Anastasia Behar: An-NUH-stay-zuh Bay-HAR

Meredith Kaesy: Mare-UH-dith KAY-see

Alixandra Bludeg: Al-ix-AN-dra BLU-deg

Creon: KREE-on

Vasileios Maeb-Somni: Va-ssee'-lee-os Mahb-SOM-nee

Shiloh Leigdraca: SHY-low Lē(d)zh-DRA-ca

PROLOGUE

Four Years Ago

The night pressed in around Lana as she hovered just outside her mother's bedroom door, that had been left slightly ajar. Dull, yellow light spilled from the doorframe. Her mother's voice floated through the crack with a panicked intensity that Lana had never heard before.

She leaned forward, struggling for a glimpse of her mother through the cracked door. Her mother, Elaine, stood in the middle of the room, at the foot of her perfectly made bed. Elaine's honey blonde hair stuck to her face in sweaty clumps and in front of her gold hazel eyes — a starburst of deep brown and gold.

Marty ran his hand over Elaine's tattoo-covered arm whispering soothing words—a sight that Lana had grown accustomed to in the last year. But her mother hadn't been this upset before. She'd never looked so terrified.

"They've found a way into this world, Martin." She pressed her hand against her lips as tears slid down her cheeks. "Nowhere is safe."

During her last year, her mother had been acting strangely, but what was she talking about? *What was coming?*

"It's okay, sweetheart. Nothing will hurt you here. It's safe," he murmured.

Her mother pushed him away. "You don't understand. Harmoni has turned." She trailed off as the tears ran rivulets down her cheeks.

"Elaine." Marty took a careful step toward her.

Lana held her breath, trying to stay silent as she made sense of the scene unfolding before her. She'd never heard the name before—Harmoni. *Who is that? What was that?* The only thing Lana ever heard her mother talking about "turning" was spoiled milk. *Why was she so upset?* Her thoughts spun.

"Silvis will be overrun, and the beasts will find their way here. I need to do something. She's not safe. My daughter isn't safe." Her voice shook with the force of a repressed sob. "I can help them, and then we can finally go home. I must try. I'm so sorry, Martin."

"Elaine, please. You're talking nonsense again. Listen to me, please," Marty begged, reaching out for her, but she stepped back, holding her hands up to keep him at bay.

Nothing made sense. Lana considered stepping into the room. *Would that help or hurt?* Her hand hovered over the doorknob as she struggled with the decision. *What could she say or do that Marty couldn't?* She wasn't supposed to be up this late, and she'd already eavesdropped so long. *Would her mother be angry with her for stepping in?*

"All this time, I've been preparing—I'd hoped it wouldn't come to this, but I've done what I can to keep you safe as possible. I love you," she said. "Don't go outside, especially past the fence, at night. Don't stand in the deep shadows. Avoid the in-between times—all in-betweens lead to Faerie. I'll come back as soon as I can, when it's safe."

Faerie? Lana wrapped her fingers around the doorknob. She had to do something. She had to help her mother. *But what could she do? What use was she?* Icy tendrils of fear held her captive.

Her mother took another step back until she stood in front of the bathroom doorway, where the shadows of the night were already dark as the space between stars.

"Come back? What do you mean? Where are you going?" Marty scanned the room, eyes catching on each of the exits—the bedroom door where Lana hid and the window; both were far away from where her mother stood.

"I'm going to Kaelum." She smiled. Sorrow lurked in the curve of her lips. "Please tell Lana that I love her. Tell her to look from the dark place."

"Elaine...I'm worried, darling. That's not real. It's in your head. Let's just get some sleep and you'll feel better in the morning."

A shimmer in the shadows caught Lana's attention, and her heart leapt into her throat. *What was happening?*

Her mother looked straight at Lana, and she swore her mother saw her there as she smiled and said, "Goodbye, my love." The shadows in the doorway to the bathroom coalesced, wobbling and shimmering like the night sky. Her mother stepped back into the dripping darkness.

Marty rushed forward, trying to grab her hand. "Elaine?! What the hell is happening? Elaine!"

Lana stood frozen in the doorway as her mother disappeared. The shadows fell away as if they'd never existed at all. Her mother was gone.

Marty scrambled, screaming her mother's name as he searched the bathroom, but the room was completely empty.

He fell to his knees, staring at the place his wife had once been, her name a terrified prayer on his lips.

Lana stumbled away from the door, too aware of the darkness that surrounded her in the hallway. She ran, chased by the sound of Marty's sobs, flicking on light switches as she went.

CHAPTER I

Lana

There were three rules that Lana lived by since her mother's disappearance four years ago:

1. Always be home before dark.

2. Never stand in the deep shadows.

3. Never linger at in-betweens, especially doorways.

So, as she left her evening shift at Mina's Diner, Lana stepped quickly through the door and hurried away from the shadow of the old building. In the white light of the street lamps, she scanned the surroundings, eyes lingering on the shadows cast by the moon creeping up the eastern sky. The diner, with its chipped paint and dirty windows—some still boarded up from the last hurricane—sat at the top of a hill that overlooked the river. Cypress trees, with their knees jutting from the lazy river current, lined the other side of the water.

Lana stared at the watchful darkness in the woods, where the branches converged. Wind stirred her hair, tugging strands free from the high ponytail she wore to work, leaving her with chills where her hair brushed against skin. Even so far away, she could smell the soapy scent of crushed magnolia leaves carried by the breeze.

The door behind her banged open. Startled by the sudden sound, her breath caught and she stumbled, stepping off the curb and into the faded parking lot of the diner.

She turned suddenly, bringing Tara's familiar face into view. She was one of the other girls who worked at the diner. Definitely not her favorite coworker. She grimaced inwardly, waiting to hear what Tara wanted.

"Lana! Wait, I need a huge favor," she said with a smile as wide as the river plastered on her face.

Of course she did. "Yes?"

"Take my shift tomorrow?" she asked, but before Lana could answer, Tara babbled out her reasons. "My new boyfriend got me tickets to the Undead Loves concert and you know it's my favorite band, so I really *really* want to go. It was so sweet of him, and you know they're so expensive, and he can't return them, so please. Pretty please. I'll grab a shift for you later, if you want."

Lana sighed. Taking Tara's shift tomorrow would put her at seven days this week, but what else was she going to do any-way? She didn't have any friends — other than Liam who she barely saw since he got into med school. Her heart clenched. She missed him. He was the only person, other than her mom and Marty, who had been constant in her life. She'd never had long time friends, never really clicked with the other kids in town. And she'd never had a boyfriend. Not that Lana didn't want a partner. She loved love. In her free time, she watched rom-coms and read sappy romance novels. She desperately wanted love, but it just wasn't for her.

She tried dating for a while, but every romance she'd ever had felt wrong somehow — gross — so she gave up on dating years ago. She grimaced as a memory filtered to the surface: in tenth grade, a boy tried to kiss her at a football game. He was cute and nice, but she didn't even know his name. He leaned in and the thought of his warm lips, wet with saliva, and too soft skin made her heart race. Lana had nearly fallen off the bleachers trying to scramble away. There was only one person she could stand being close to, but he would never see her the way she saw him. But her quiet feelings were a secret, as they had been for over a decade. They were *just* friends.

"Sure," Lana said, finally.

Tara squealed and then ran back inside without another word. Alone again, Lana trudged toward her car. The streetlight buzzed overhead, flickering. With each flicker, the shadows seemed to move, crawling closer to her. Undulating with malice.

Lana quickened her pace. She'd had to park all the way by the treeline when she clocked in — too many customers, which she guessed was a good thing for Mina, but not so much for her. Goosebumps crawled along her arms.

The light flickered again, going dark for an entire second. Red eyes glowed in the woods. A howl broke through the air and Lana screamed as she broke into a full out run to her car.

In the woods in front of her car, the shadows converged, warbling between two trees. Just like the night her mother disappeared. Breathing heavily, Lana fumbled with her keys. She jammed her finger on the button. Click. Unlocked.

Unable to stop her momentum, Lana crashed against the car door. She rolled to the side and ripped the door open. In a fluid movement, she was inside with the door slammed shut and locked. She flicked on the headlights, which bathed part of the lot and the woods beyond.

Nothing was there. No living shadows. No red eyes. Nothing.

Lana took deep, ragged breaths. Was it in her head? Was she *that* sleep deprived? It must be her imagination, she reasoned. But a nagging voice in the back of her said it wasn't, reminded her of the night her mother disappeared. Instead of examining her thoughts any more, Lana threw her car in reverse and hurriedly left the parking lot.

She drove straight home. The car jostled down the dirt drive way. Ancient live oak trees, dripping with moss, surrounded the house, which nestled in four acres of woods—an inheritance from her mother's side of the family. Only the side of the property facing the road was bereft of trees. It was a large house and looked like it belonged in an old *Southern Living* magazine. At least, it would if the place wasn't falling apart from neglect.

Ever since her mother disappeared, Marty, her stepfather, had stopped tending to it, other than occasionally mowing the grass closest to the house. Black sooty mold grew on the white siding from pollen that was never washed off.

The solid board fence was the cleanest thing on the property—mostly because it was the newest. Five years ago, her mother had insisted on a sturdy wooden fence around the house and the trees cut back farther from the yard. Lana spent most of her days helping her mother string up lanterns that stretched from the fence to the house. She'd initially thought her mother was preparing for some elaborate party, but that thought evaporated when she noticed her mother burying strange objects in the ground and weaving golden thread along the perimeter of the fence.

Lana only asked once what her mother was doing, and Elaine had simply responded, "I'm protecting you." Lana never asked again. But she began to pay more attention. She'd listened at their bedroom door the night her mother disappeared. She heard every word, kept them stashed in the back of her mind as nightmare fodder with all the other things that made no sense—like the rules and the fence.

Lana blinked away the memories and turned the car off. Every single light was on in the house, including the lanterns that were strung across the yard. The lights were always on, even in the middle of the day. It had been that way since the night her mother disappeared.

Still haunted by whatever had happened — or hadn't happened — at the diner that night, Lana threw the car door open and made a run for the safety of the house. Bright lights were safe. The monsters didn't like the light. Once safe in the house, she leaned against the closed door and steadied her breathing. The overhead lights stung her eyes after driving in the dark, but the nice thing about having every light on in the house meant she didn't need to stop and flip switches. Though, she did wonder about the electric bill, but that didn't matter. Her mother's family left them with a large inheritance and they'd been paying bills from that for years.

Spurred on by her grumbling stomach, Lana wandered into the kitchen and began digging through the cabinets for a snack. Her eyes drifted to the corner of the room, where the microwave hung over the stove, creating a pocket of darkness despite the overhead lights.

The shadows seemed to move along the black glass stove-top. Her nightmares rushed to the forefront of her mind again, freezing her in place. "It's not real," she said to reassure herself. Shadows don't move, not like that. It's just my imagination, she reasoned, but she still warred with her pounding heart.

"It's not real," she said again. She needed more sleep. Exhaustion was making her illogical. What she saw the night her mother left was illogical. What she saw outside of the diner was illogical. No matter how much she tried to reason with herself, she knew the truth. She'd seen the truth when her mother disappeared. The shadows were dangerous. She took a deep breath and shoved her fears to the back of her mind. In the house, she was safe. Nothing could hurt her here.

"Hey," said Marty. Lana jumped, slamming the cabinet shut as she whirled around to her stepdad, tearing her wide eyes away from that dark corner. She hadn't heard him come in. His eyes scanned the kitchen. Lana knew he was looking for the shadows too. She'd heard him screaming in his sleep, caught in some nightmare, murmuring her mother's name, pleading for her to come back, to save him.

She wondered whether, in his nightmares, he saw the same things she did.

Lana finally managed a response. "Hey."

He looked at her with bloodshot eyes and a raised brow, swaying as if caught by some breeze. It didn't surprise Lana that he was already drunk—she honestly couldn't remember when she'd seen him sober in the last few years. Not that she blamed him.

She shrugged, responding to his questioning brow. "It's nothing. I just had a long shift." They didn't talk about the shadows, or the night Mom disappeared. Shifting back and forth, Lana decided to ask something she'd never asked before. "What happened that night?"

His face paled, and he shook his head. "I don't know what you mean, Lana."

"With Mom."

He shook his head again. The few strands of hair on his head shuddered with the movement.

"There's got to be some way to find out, right?"

Marty turned his back on her, clutching his temple with one hand. "Your mom left us. That's all that happened." He stepped into the hallway.

"What about her stuff? Did she say anything? What about ..." Lana hesitated on the word she'd never let fall from her lips. "Kaelum?"

Marty stiffened. His fingers trembled at his side. "If you want to look through her books, they're in her room." Since Mom disappeared, Marty had moved out of their bedroom into an empty one down the hall. Neither of them had entered that room in four years, but, finally, Lana decided she would. Tomorrow. When the morning light filtered in the big windows and banished any possibility of shadows.

With a deep sigh, Marty lumbered away. The floor boards creaking beneath his considerable weight.

Alone again, weariness reared its head. Lana trudged up the stairs to her room, grateful that the lights left no shadows to taunt her. She was exhausted, but her stomach tightened with dread. If she slept, the nightmares would find her. She couldn't sleep, no matter how much she wanted to.

Her room wasn't nearly as bright as the other rooms in the house. She kept only one lamp by the window. She flicked the overhead light on, banishing the few shadows that remained.

After a momentary debate, Lana climbed into bed. Closing her eyes for a few minutes wouldn't hurt. She wouldn't sleep, just rest for a little bit, but the weight of her exhaustion drew her in with sweet promises of rest.

With her head buried against a pillow, Lana fell into the dark of sleep.

CHAPTER 2

Lana

As Lana sank into sleep, the safety of the lights faded away, and the bed beneath her became the hot sand of endless dunes in a desert landscape lit only by the dying sun. She was in her most familiar nightmare—the twilight desert of the beasts, a place of rotting flesh and blood-soaked wastes.

Lana jolted up from the ground, struggling against the sand that threatened to pull her under. In the distance, flashes of fire flickered. *Fire.* Lana exhaled in relief. The safest place in the desert was by the fire. The monsters hated light, so she ran.

As she approached, the fire grew larger. The unhindered flames darted across wooden buildings that crumbled beneath the heat. Lana slowed her step. The sand became firmer, like stone. With the knowing of dreams, she understood that this village was the only one across the entire desert and had been empty for decades—just like the temple it was connected to.

A familiar voice screamed, piercing the night—anger and loss intermingling in the sound. Her body acted of its own accord, pushing her toward the sound. Lana ran until a woman's figure became visible among the flames and smoke.

The tall, muscled woman wore intricate metal armor that reflected the flames. A red and gold crest splayed across her chest. Entranced by the knight, Lana halted, watching the woman, whose ashen hair waved in the breeze that fueled the flames, despite the braids tucked tight behind her pointed ears.

A man in similar armor stood at the edge of the village, keeping his distance from the hungry fire. "We need to leave!"

"I won't rest," she said, "until I find Meredith or every last Hollow is dead."

"General Bludeg, you can't kill them all!" The soldier fidgeted in place, looking back to the horizon where a wave of shadowy dots undulated in the moonlight.

Lana clenched her hands to her chest. *The monsters—Hollows. They were coming.* She couldn't tear her eyes from the horizon, where the distant figures only drew closer with every breath. Memories of their mottled flesh, wrapped in shadow, of their glowing red eyes, flashed in Lana's mind, and terror churned in her stomach.

"We can't take on an entire horde," the soldier said, pleading with the general.

"Let them come." General Bludeg pulled her sword from its sheath. "I have a promise to keep." She bared her teeth, snarling as she waved her sword in the air toward the incoming Hollows. "Come get me, beasts!"

The soldier turned tail and ran, leaving Lana alone with the fearless general. In this nightmare, Lana was always a ghost. The general couldn't see her, couldn't hear her. Lana could only stand and watch, terrified but unable to avert her gaze from the horror the general would soon face.

Despite knowing she was in her nightmares, Lana couldn't ignore the fear that urged her to hide. She scrambled up stone steps and took shelter at the top of a nearby building—one of the few made entirely of stone. She crouched in her perch, watching as the monsters descended.

The Hollows appeared, swarming the ruined village like a plague. Bodies like rotting wolves, twisted bones jutting through sparse fur, all covered in smoke and wrapped in red lightning that jolted around their bodies. Eyes glowing with that same red magic. With them came the strengthening scent of decay. Their bodies jerked unpredictably, the sand shifting beneath their feet in unnatural ways.

They howled, snapping their hungry teeth; foamy spit splattered on the ground. Like water twisting into a whirlpool, the Hollows circled General Bludeg, who swung with hateful precision, cutting down each monster that dared draw close. Her blade cut through necks with ease, leaving the Hollows crumpled on the ground, bleeding brown-black blood.

Despite her prowess, the beasts kept coming. Lana could do nothing but watch the nightmare play out before her. Though her heart beat wildly, begging her to do something, to somehow save General Bludeg from certain death.

The general climbed over bodies, feet squelching in enemy flesh, ready to meet her attackers, but the Hollows pressed closer, tightening around the general. She sank to a knee, breath coming in quick bursts.

Lana shoved to her feet, already moving to the stairs.

The beasts lunged and buried the general beneath the heap of their twisting flesh and fangs. Not even a wisp of her could be seen.

Lana's eyes widened as the air rushed from her chest in a sudden cry. *Alix. No. No. Please.* She could barely breathe as she ran to the heap of monsters. Sobbing, she shoved her hands in, desperate to rip them away, but Lana was useless. Her ghostly hands passed through their flesh. She could do nothing.

The ground shook and red light flared up from the pile of beasts as a wave of sand exploded and engulfed them all, pulling Lana down with them. She screamed as sand covered her face and filled her mouth and nose. Lana thrashed and fought against the desert, but it consumed her until only darkness was left.

Lana fell through the ground, something that had never happened before. She was at the whims of the desert, jerked through caves and dark passages as if by magic. Shadows and soft blue light danced around her, but the magic moved her too quickly. It was all a blur, until she stopped. As the magic suddenly released her, she stumbled into an open room — a ruined library.

Towering shelves of books loomed over her, somehow pristine despite the state of everything else. Broken furniture. A thick layer of dust covering everything. Everything except the books and their shelves. Muttering filtered past all of the shelves, a quiet, feminine sound.

Lana followed the sound. In the corner, a woman bent over a desk, which was cluttered with stacks of books and crumpled papers. The woman swore and scratched through a line of words in her notebook. She plopped backwards in her chair and her hair slid away from her face. Blonde hair — the same shade as Lana's. And her eyes were a familiar starburst golden hazel.

Mom.

Lana rushed forward and threw her arms around her mother, but her arms slid through Elaine's body, and Lana fell, sprawling on the cold ground. She scrunched up her eyes as she picked herself off the ground. Why couldn't she hug her mom, even in a dream?

"Mom," she said with a trembling voice, but Elaine didn't turn.

Lana grabbed at her hands, but still she couldn't touch her. "Mom," she cried. Over and over again, Lana cried out to her mother who couldn't hear her. She was merely a ghost, floating in a dream. Her mother still lost amid the torment of Lana's nightmares.

Lana crumpled to the ground, staring up at her mother, who continued reading and scribbling in her notebooks without realizing her daughter sat at her feet.

Lana woke with a start, tears flooding down her cheeks. Morning light glittered in the window.

Marty's concerned face hovered above her own. "It's okay, Lana. It's all right. You're safe, now." He brushed a hand across her hair, his frown deepening the creases in his brow and cheeks.

The familiar reek of beer radiated from him, and Lana exhaled slowly. *She was home.* Her body shuddered with a sob. "I'm all right," she said between breaths.

"All right then." He leaned away. "All right." Marty shuffled back to her bedroom door with a haunted understanding in his eyes.

Lana stared after him as he left. She took deep breaths to calm her racing heart. *Only a dream.* She wiped the tears from her face and forced the images from her mind, refusing to think about what she'd seen. Dwelling on the nightmares never eliminated them, never soothed her. She'd learned it was best to forget.

So instead, she focused on her plans for the day. She wouldn't ignore what happened four years ago anymore. Her mother had left secrets that Lana was determined to uncover. Today, she would finally look through whatever clues her mother had left behind. One way or another, she'd figure out if what she saw that night was real, or if she was really losing her mind.

Lana rubbed tiredness from her eyes and stood in front of the mirror, taking longer than usual to tame her hair. She studied herself; the bags under her eyes couldn't be helped, so she swiped mascara through her lashes to frame her dark eyes, hoping that would be enough to look normal. Despite her attempts, Lana couldn't release the uneasy feeling of creatures in the shadows, watching and waiting.

CHAPTER 3

Vasileios — 25 Years Ago in Kaelum

Last year, archaeologists from the royal academy uncovered a wellspring, unleashing a tidal wave of magic on the lands of Silvis for the first time in centuries, where only a trickle had been before. With more magic came rumors of the Hollows, reborn into Kaelum after their defeat in the Dae Era. Everyone knew the legends of Dae, the Savior of Silvis, and feared magic as the source of all suffering, but no one dared believe the nightmares could return.

The bustle of anxiety filled the once calm and empty halls of the palace. Nobles took up residence in the palace, hoping for safety far away from the desert island at the center of the kingdom, where Hollows were said to congregate at the wellspring. More servants were hired or brought on by the noble guests. Knights were stationed at every entryway and patrolled the grounds.

No matter where he went—his room, the library, even a broom closet—Vas felt surrounded. He could hear their chatter through the walls. Laughter and footsteps clattered down the hallways. He couldn't stand it.

It had been centuries since the shadow monsters had roamed Silvis, and, now, Vas heard whispers of war. The nobles were calling it the Hollow War, but how could it be a war when they were fighting against mindless beasts?

Unlike the other fae, Vas was intrigued by the new rush of magic. In Kaelum, magic never truly disappeared, but until the wellspring was uncovered, magic had been a quiet hum in the pit of his stomach. Now, it was a roar, rushing through his veins, begging to be unleashed. He finally felt alive, joined with the land around him. He yearned to learn all he could, so he became stealthy.

Slipping away from the servants had been particularly easy today, which Vas chalked up to the upcoming social season. He stuck to the safety of the shadows as he slipped into the front courtyard, full of roses in a rainbow of colors. Rosemary perfumed the air, mixing with the cloying aroma of honeysuckle.

The center of the garden held a two-tiered, stone fountain, ringed with red roses—always in full bloom. No matter the season, or the state of the rest of the garden, those roses never wilted. The fountain itself was pitiful. Barely a puddle of water sat in the basin, but no one bothered with it. His mother kept it exactly the way it was.

Vas quickened his pace, heading toward the edge of the courtyard, where oak and pine clumped together in a little wilderness that helped insulate the palace from the outside world—the bustling city beyond, the mountains in the distance, the desert at the heart of Silvis, and the human city of Haven beneath it.

Other than servants and guards, Vas was so isolated in the palace that he'd only read about places beyond Silvis, like the other faerie courts in Kaelum, the faerie realms beyond Kaelum, and the mundane world, where the Havenites had come from.

He was halfway to the safety of the shrubs that would conceal his entrance to the woods, when he heard the bubbling voices of the courtiers. He pulled his hood tighter over his white hair and curling ram horns that marked him as different from the Silvids.

While Silvid fae looked as human as the Havenites, other than their slightly pointed ears, Vas was half-Brynian and looked part animal with dark horns curling, like a ram's, from the white curls of his hair. Powerful Brynians, his father once told him, were sometimes born with animalistic attributes—that it was something to be proud of. But Vas had never met anyone with animal parts, not even his Brynian prince of a father. Vas felt like a disgusting divergence. Before his thoughts could spiral further, he lengthened his stride, making his way to the tree line, hoping to blend in with the shadows.

"Oh, look, there goes the goat prince," said a laughing voice, floating on the floral breeze. The comment sent the other courtiers nearby into fits of mocking laughter.

Vas ducked his head, pulling on his cloak. *Ignore them. Ignore them.* In his youth, he went to his mother and tattled on the cruel comments of the courtiers, but that had only ended with him standing in front of the entire court, while his mother went on a rage-fueled tirade that ended with the two offenders forced to clean the stables for months. That entire year, the nobles looked at him with sneers and snide comments from a distant, too terrified of manual labor to approach him.

Vas was there when the two were released from their labor. Looking at them had made him nauseous—their dainty figures dirty and disheveled, scowls deeper and filled with a deep resentment. His mother's punishment had only made them more hateful. Ever since then, Vas didn't mention anything to his parents—the queen of Silvis and her king consort. He'd rather ignore the bullying. It didn't take long before the courtiers realized he wouldn't say anything and they began teasing him again—of course, only in the safety of the courtyards and hallways when his parents and most loyal servants weren't around. No one wanted a prince like him.

Times like these, Vas was glad he'd convinced his mother to let him delay his debut in society. He didn't think he could withstand the judgmental looks he'd certainly get at any of the fae dances. Being pranced about during the social season would only be a repeat of his humiliation. At twenty-four, he hoped his mother would continue to indulge him, if only for a few more years.

Finally, Vas stepped into the wilderness, blending in with the overgrowth. He took a familiar path through the trees and bushes to a small clearing by the stone wall that surrounded the palace. Light filtered past the dark-green leaves of the treetops. Vas slid through a cluster of dogwoods and sat against the trunk of an old pine, not caring whether turpentine stained his cloak. The smell wrapped around him, a comfort, as he pulled a dusty book from under his cloak.

A white-throated sparrow chirped nearby, and Vas felt like he could finally breathe. *Alone at last.* Vas brushed a layer of dust from the old, cracked leather cover of the book. He traced the golden embossed letters of the title—*Brynian Theory of Illusion and Shape.* The spine creaked as he opened the prize that he'd stolen from his father's study. Shifting had been the only magic his mother had allowed him to learn, and only then because his father had argued he needed connection to his Brynian roots, the magic of his people. She only gave in when she realized shifting could be a wonderful means of escape if danger ever broke out.

But his shifting lessons had long been over. His mother denied him anything else, fearing it would corrupt his soul, or that perhaps a Hollow would sense his magic and come to consume it. But Hollows weren't ever seen this far inland. She was overreacting, and Vas felt confident his father wouldn't notice the missing book.

He flipped through the chapters, scanning some he'd already read about shifting. He had no interest in those—Vas could shift into almost any animal he could think of, no matter the size. What he was hoping to find was a passage about permanent shifting—something to permanently shift away his horns, so the court would accept him, but shifting his fae shape was too advanced, even for him.

Fae-shape shifting, also called skin shifting, was a thing of legends. Vas let his mind wander as he flipped through the pages. What chaos could someone cause if they could shape their face to look like anyone, to change themselves so completely? He stopped on a page. "Fae-shape Shifting Theory." He skimmed the page, shaking his head. The theory behind fae-shape shifting didn't make sense to Vas at all. It should be similar to bestial forms, especially considering all Brynian magic was basically an illusion anyway—a temporary mask. What was so complicated about a face that it couldn't be illusioned away?

Vas thumbed through the book, skipping to later chapters. His breath caught in his throat as a piece of paper fluttered to the ground. Fearing he'd accidentally ripped a page from the book, he scrambled to grab the paper before the damp dirt could ruin it. He held up the paper, realizing it was already ruined, water and mud smeared across the brittle page. It seemed much older than the book he was holding. Guilt rushed through him as he held the messed-up page, reading what was left of the contents.

The Hollows and the ... being the only obstacle to the peaceful rule ... Magic—the source of the Hollows, their hunger and birth ... And so we sealed away the ... to repress the beast is to be free ... We shattered the bonds of the Hollow pack and ... Of Dreams and Nightmares—the court became two. Long live King Dae of the New Court of Dreams.

A page from the histories? Not knowing what else to do, Vas tucked the page into the back of the book again. Maybe his father wouldn't notice. To distract himself, Vas turned back to his study.

He spent hours in quiet contemplation, carefully flipping through page after page of magical theories and spells. Nothing he found could get rid of his hated horns. He hated the ridges that scraped his fingers, the matte black of them that reminded him of dark corners at night, and the perfect unbroken curves that came to a point beneath his ears. Pushing away his despair, Vas leaned down, pressing his nose into the book to take a deep, calming inhale. The bovine stench of the parchment cleared his head for a moment.

When his parents finally abdicated the throne, he needed the Silvids to accept him. He had to find a way to be normal. *Just keep reading.* He would find a solution somewhere in the pages—an illusion to hide his features, or some theory of fae-shape shifting he could actually manage. Anything to just be like all the other fae.

Vas forced himself to refocus on the passage he was reading about illusions. He'd already read about mental and emotional manipulation, and now he was caught on a page about visual illusion—a duplication illusion spell. It wasn't what he was looking for, but his curiosity about this forbidden knowledge held him on the page. He held out his hand, attempting to replicate the gestures described. He twisted his hand, twirling his fingers as if grasping something in the air.

"Gee-fehn-lay-cahn," he whispered, but nothing happened. Not even a flicker.

Vas sighed. Shifting was so much easier. He'd never needed words or ridiculous hand movements, something his father had called "remarkable" and "genius." Slipping into another shape was like breathing for him—why couldn't he shift away his horns?

A twig snapped feet away from where Vas still hid, concealed by the dogwoods.

"Prince Vasileios," a familiar voice called out. Athan—his father's advisor.

In an instant, Vas's body began to shift, the book forgotten on the ground with a thud. He exhaled as his body twisted into the shape of a cardinal and he fluttered to a nearby oak branch, perching just out of reach.

"You should know your whispers are quite loud, my prince." Athan stood straight and tall, wrapped in his elegant robes. He looked the perfect Silvid courtier—dark hair and even darker eyes, with ears that curved into a delicate point. He wore a careful smile, one that hinted at the foxlike cunning that won him his spot as advisor to the king consort. "Come now, Prince. I know you're still here. You may be a talented shifter, but I can still see you."

At that moment, Athan's eyes swung upward and caught on Vas, whose heart thundered in his chest with the urgency to run, to hide.

"Ah. There you are, delightful little bird. I do wonder what you've been up to, whispering strange words in secret." Athan's words trailed off as he approached the bushes where Vas had been hiding just moments earlier.

Realization hit Vas like a wave of dread—the stolen book of magic still sat on the ground behind those bushes. He dropped from the tree, shifting as he fell. His body expanded, bones shifting and reforming. In a single breath, Vas was himself once again, and crouching on the ground.

Unfortunately, Athan stood between Vas and the book. With a mischievous grin, Athan slipped behind the bushes.

"Wait!" Vas called, jumping out of his crouch with an outstretched hand, as if to snatch Athan away.

Ignoring Vas's plea, Athan retrieved the book and stepped out of the bushes, his eyes dancing with amusement. "I thought I'd heard you butchering illusions," he teased.

Vas's hands fell to his sides in shock. A Silvid shouldn't recognize Brynian words of magic. "What?"

Athan tossed the book to Vas, who fumbled to catch it before pulling it tight against his chest.

"You and I are more alike than you know." Athan brushed stray leaves from his robes.

Alike? How? Was Athan as curious about magic as he was? Vas's thoughts raced, trying to make connections he'd never considered before. "You've read the book?" Vas finally asked.

"I have." Athan smiled slightly, his eyes sparkling at the secret they now shared.

Vas paused as he processed Athan's admission. The trees swayed around them in the gentle breeze, carrying the distinctly green scent of the forest. The birds no longer sang. Only the rustling leaves broke the silence.

"But," Vas said, "Silvids don't use the same magic as Brynians. Why read a book on Brynian magic that you can't even use?" He looked down at the book and back to Athan.

Athan shrugged. "Silvids can't create illusions. Brynians can't shape the natural world. But, everyone can read and gather knowledge for knowledge's sake. It's natural to be curious, no?"

Natural to be curious? No. His mother certainly wouldn't agree with Athan there. Silvids weren't curious. They couldn't be. Curiosity about magic was dangerous, according to his mother. Vas furrowed his brows, unsure what to make of Athan now—not that he ever knew him. His father's closest advisor spoke often, with a closed-lip, cordial smile, but never of his opinions—Vas assumed he saved those for private counsel with his father. To Vas, Athan was a mystery and always had been.

"Silvids hate magic. They don't even use their gifts anymore," Vas said.

Athan tilted his head thoughtfully. "Correct. Many do hate magic to the point of shunning their natural gifts."

"And you?" Vas asked. The silence was heavy with anticipation. Without thinking, he took a step toward Athan, closing the distance between them.

"I suppose I'm unusual. I don't fear magic." Athan's voice was barely above a whisper, letting the quiet forest hold his secret.

A lightness blossomed in Vas's chest at this unexpected similarity. His words spilled out. "But do you use it? Your magic? I've never seen it before. I've always wanted to. Silvid magic is—"

Athan held up a hand, a smile playing on his lips, and Vas closed his mouth with a nod.

"The better question is, have you?" Athan lowered his voice even further to a conspiratorial whisper. "Have you used Silvid magic?"

"Could I? I—" Vas stuttered, clutching the book tighter against his chest. His thoughts froze with a fluttering in his stomach. "I'm not really a Silvid. I'm just—"

"Your Brynian blood may be strong. You may look Brynian, but you have your mother's blood too. You are as Silvid as me, as any other Silvid."

Vas felt stupid for never considering the possibility that his mother's magic might be inside him just as much as his father's. "I wouldn't know how. Do you?" Vas spoke in a breathless rush. "Could you teach me?"

"Perhaps."

Athan's eyes glinted with an excitement that Vas couldn't place, but it left him feeling uneasy, caught between curious delight and dread.

Athan whispered, in a hushed, eager tone, "The queen would be furious if she found out you were learning magic. You know how they are—believing magic is more dangerous than ignorance. Are you willing to take that risk?"

"I—" Vas's heart thumped, rattling against his sternum. The thought of the power of Silvis flowing quietly in his veins—the ability to shape the world, to bend the ground he stood upon, to pull water from thin air, create mist, stitch together wounds—mesmerized him. That magic was real—concrete, permanent change. *What could he do with that power? Could he shape himself in the way ancient Silvid healers could regrow limbs and close wounds? Could he finally be rid of his horns forever?*

Athan waited, the grin plastered to his face showing the points of his canines.

His expression created a drumbeat of emotions—elation, uneasy, fear, excitement. A chill ran across Vas's skin, but he nodded, unable to speak his betrayal.

Athan lifted his chin and clapped once. "Perfect. I know just the place—quiet, away from the guards."

In a rush, Athan led Vas to a place on the outer wall of the palace where the vines grew thick and wild. Behind the vines sat a wrought-iron door, barely wide enough for Vas to fit. Greenery, woven into a mat, covered it perfectly.

"A secret passage?" Vas asked.

"Quite astute," Athan said. "An escape route that leads into the thickest part of the woods surrounding the palace. Useless if a fire were to break out, but potentially lifesaving in the event of a coup or other such nonsense. Only the queen, king consort, the captain of the palace guards, the queen's advisor, myself, and now you, know of this door."

Athan gestured for Vas to step through the door and into the woods on the other side.

Technically, Vas was still on the palace grounds, but even so, this was the farthest he'd ever been before. His heart raced with a freedom he'd never known.

Athan's wolfish smile fell away until he wore the familiar mask that Vas had known all these years before. "Meet me here tomorrow morning, and be sure you aren't followed."

Without waiting for Vas to respond, Athan turned and disappeared, making his way back into the manicured hedges of the palace garden.

CHAPTER 4

Vasileios — 25 Years Ago in Kaelum

The morning sun warmed Vas's skin as he sat in the little clearing beyond the iron door with Athan standing a few paces away, hands clasped in front of him.

"Brynian magic and Silvid magic differ in many ways," Athan said.

"Yes. I know." Vas choked back a sigh. He didn't need the basics. He'd read all about magic long ago. When he asked Athan to teach him, he'd wanted something more.

"Do you? Tell me, then." Athan crossed his arms, waiting for Vas to recite his knowledge.

"Brynian magic is illusion magic that only fae from the northern kingdom of Brynia can cast using words and gestures."

"Why?" Athan interjected.

Vas shifted against the tree, digging his fingers into the grass around him as he searched his mind for an answer. "Because it's not intuitive elemental magic, like Silvid magic?"

Athan shook his head before regaining his previous lecturing posture—hands clasped at his stomach and his chin held high. "Incorrect. Casting style is based on the magic source. Brynian magic uses spoken words or sigils because it harnesses the magic in the environment and therefore needs a conduit to manifest the caster's intentions."

He paced slowly in the grass, continuing his lecture. "Silvid magic, on the other hand, uses the magic inherent in the caster's soul. A Silvid mage is the conduit, their thoughts the guide for the spell.

"Kaelum, like all the other fae realms, is, itself, magic and therefore everything within it either is magical or becomes so through exposure. Of course, some locations have greater concentrations of magic, which usually forms the wellsprings."

Athan glanced at Vas, making sure he was still listening, which of course he was. Vas slid to the ground, letting his gaze wander to the sky and the clouds gently floating by.

"If you have no intention of taking these lessons seriously, Prince, then there is no need for me to waste my time." Athan clapped his hands together.

"What about the other fae courts? Where do their magics come from?"

Athan tilted his head, considering Vas with curiosity. "Though that's a bit irrelevant to our study, I'll indulge you," he said with a genuinely warm smile. "Many use a mix of sources. The Summer Court draws magic from the flame within themselves for battle magic, but their scholars are known for powerful defensive sigils. The Abyssal Court is much the same, though souls are their specialty, not only to power their magic but as the Court of Death..." He shrugged. "Fae of most of the other courts can use both, depending on their intentions. Magical source is the foundation of magical theory. I'm concerned you neglected the foundations in your independent studies."

Vas shaded his eyes from the morning sun as he continued to stare up at the sky. "I'm sure I've read it before, but must have forgotten. I've always wondered what the other courts are like."

"I'm sure that must have been the case, my prince, but you must not forget. Source is one of the most important concepts. Souls can be drained to the point of death. The land can be drained of magic to famine. Knowing your source and what it's capable of is of the utmost importance. Now. Tell me, why is Brynian magic illusory with environmental source?"

"Brynia has more wellsprings than we do, and, so, they have greater stores of magic outside of themselves than within?" Vas lifted his head, trying to read Athan's expression. *Was he correct?* With the reassurance of his teacher's subtle nod, Vas dropped his head back to the warm grass.

Surrounded by the earthy smell of bruised grass, Vas inhaled and spoke his curiosity aloud, "So, can Brynians use a soul source?"

Athan hesitated. The breeze rustled the canopy in the beat of silence before he answered, "Well, yes, but illusions are complicated. It's not advisable to power them with your soul, though I'll admit I've never heard what happens if a Brynian burns through the magic in their soul. Death, likely, I suppose."

Another stretch of silence held them captive in the meadow before Athan continued with another question. "What is the Brynian court?" He began to pace across the clearing again with his hands clasped before him.

"How is this related to magic?" Vas pushed up onto his elbows.

Athan raised his brows. "Am I not your teacher? Do you not trust I will teach you?"

An embarrassed flush heated Vas's cheeks, and he sat up straight, crossing his legs beneath him. "I trust you."

Athan smiled, a quiet fondness in his eyes, despite the sharpness that always lurked there.

Vas didn't know what to think. *Why was Athan taking time to teach him? Had his father requested these secret lessons?*

"Prince Vasileios, what court is in Brynia?" Athan asked again.

"The Wild Court," Vas said. The morning breeze swirled through the clearing, ruffling Vas's hair.

"And what was it before then?" Athan paused his pacing, waiting with that quiet smile.

"I don't know." Vas had never known of it as anything else. Did he pay so little attention in history lessons? Court names were important enough that he should have learned something like this already.

"The Court of Dreams." Athan stood still, as if expecting a reaction from Vas, but Vas merely furrowed his brow.

"But Silvis is the Court of Dreams."

"But it hasn't always been." Athan began his pacing again, chin tilted to the sky. "In ancient times, Brynia and Silvis were one land, one court—the Court of Dreams *and* Nightmares. Like the Summer Court, they used both sources of magic, soul and environment." Athan slowed, his eyes growing distant as he stared into the shadows of the woods around them. "The land was split in two—Silvis was broken from the continent, becoming an island on its own. So, the court split as well—the Court of Dreams in Brynia and the Court of Nightmares in Silvis. War broke out, of course, which King Dae ended with the eradication of the Hollows and a treaty that renamed the courts. Brynia became the Court of Wild Dreams and Silvis the Court of New Dreams, which eventually became just the Wild Court and the Court of Dreams."

Athan fell silent, still staring into the distant darkness of the trees.

Vas watched him, contemplating this strange lecture. *What was Athan trying to tell him, to teach him with this history?*

"What happened to the Court of Nightmares?" Vas trailed his finger through the grass in front of him.

"The First War and the treaty included the sealing of the wellspring in Silvis. During the war, Silvids came to believe magic to be the source of suffering for their people—remember how Silvid magic uses the caster's soul as the source? The war meant many were losing their lives to the cost of their own magic. King Dae had the wellspring sealed; a treaty was made and the war ended. The Hollows disappeared. Thus, the Court of Nightmares perished."

Vas still didn't quite understand. He bit at the dry skin of his bottom lip, trying to put the pieces together. "The Hollows were the Court of Nightmares?"

Athan shrugged. "I suppose, something like that. The histories from that time are not entirely intact. Interesting, no?"

"But, what does it have to do with magic?" Vas finally asked.

"Everything. Are you not of both courts?" Athan took a step closer to Vas and into the shade of the oak tree.

"Well, yes," Vas said.

"The history of both courts is the history of magic in Kaelum." Athan nodded sagely. "And since your lineage is from both courts, this knowledge is a necessary foundation to your magical study."

"History isn't very practical. I want to learn something I can actually use."

Athan laughed, shaking his head. "Impatient prince. Fine, an illusion might sate your curiosity. Repeat this word: *Geefenlaecan.*"

Vas sat straighter with eagerness at finally learning some real magic. "*Geefenlaecan.*" His eyes lit up. "This is the spell I was trying to learn when you found me yesterday!" Hearing Athan say the spell out loud, Vas realized he had absolutely butchered the pronunciation.

"It is." Athan smiled softly. "Then, this should come easily. Focus on the intention for the spell as you say the word. See it in your mind's eye as if it is already happening."

"What about the hand gesture?"

Athan shook his head. "Old texts give gestures, but any mage worth his robes can do it without them. Feel free to use the gesture if you need the focus, I suppose." He stepped several paces back and waited.

Vas focused, recalling the purpose of the spell—duplication. It was an illusion that copied himself to disorient an attacker or amuse a crowd. Likely useless, but the spell had caught his eye when he'd been reading his father's book. Curiosity had always been one of Vas's weaknesses.

"*Geefenlaecan.*" Vas tried to imagine another copy of himself, kneeling on the grass beside him, but nothing happened.

He scrunched up his brows in concentration, trying to will the illusion into existence as he spoke the word again: "*Geefenlaecan.*"

"Hmm." Athan walked in a half-circle around Vas. "Tap into your magic—the thrum of magic beating in the world around you."

Vas closed his eyes, trying to find the trickle of energy around him. His father had taught him to do this when he'd been learning shifting, but it'd been so easy then. He'd felt the magic like a heartbeat inside himself; even without the words, he'd been able to shift.

Vas splayed his hands in the grass and suddenly he felt it: the steady pulse of magic in every single blade of grass. He inhaled slowly, pulling the magic from the grass around his hand. Like a wave, it rushed in, flooding him, and he sighed at the pleasant tingle along his arm.

"Prince, I believe that's a bit much. You need more practice than I thought." Athan put a hand on his shoulder to jostle Vas out of his reverie.

When Vas opened his eyes, he was shocked at the sight before him. The once beautifully green grass he'd been sitting in was completely dead—brown as it had been in the middle of winter. "Oh no," Vas said, his heart falling. "I didn't mean to. The grass—"

"The grass will be just fine, given some time." Athan cut him off. "Let's return to the palace. I expect you to study in between lessons. In the library, there are several books I'd like you to find and begin reading."

Athan began listing books as they made their way back through the secret passage in the palace walls, but Vas merely nodded along, lost in thought. Learning magic seemed like it was going to be significantly harder than shifting had been. He grit his teeth. If he could master a spell to conceal his horns, it would all be worth it. He just hoped Athan would be able to help him with that.

CHAPTER 5

Lana

Lana stood in front of the door to her mother's room. Her fingers brushed against the doorknob, hesitant and uncertain. Was she really going to do this? What did she expect to find? Steeling herself against her memories, she twisted the knob and pushed. The door creaked open, squealing on hinges that hadn't been used in four long years.

It was exactly the same as it always had been. A king size bed in the middle of the room with a blue comforter smoothed over the bed, still made and unused. The bathroom door stood open a few steps from the foot of the bed. Images of that night flashed before Lana's eyes. The shadows gathering in that doorway, sparkling like the night sky. Her mother stepping back. Disappearing. Leaving them. Why?

Stumbling backwards, Lana clutched at her shirt over her heart. Tears burned at the corner of her eyes, but she had to do this. She needed to know the truth. What had she seen that night? With a deep breath, Lana dropped her hands and stepped into the room. The musty scent of the unused room met her, only reminding her of the time she'd wasted until now.

At the far side of the room, her mother's desk sat by a large window, which filled the room with bright natural light. Lana crept closer. Much like the desk from her dream, this one was stacked with papers and books. She leaned over, narrowing her eyes at the words on each page. She couldn't read it. Strange squiggles and symbols that somehow looked familiar but were completely illegible, and unrecognizable. She imagined for a moment that her mother must have learned Tolkein's elvish just to write secret notes to herself, but she quickly dismissed that idea. Her mother had never even watched LOTR.

With a shaky breath, Lana sat on her mother's desk chair and sifted through the papers, making little piles. One stack for the foreign language. One stack for English. Glancing at the ones she could actually read, Lana's heart sank. They were grocery lists. To-do lists. Completely mundane items that didn't explain anything about that night. She tossed a few of those to the side, stopping on a page with a mix of English and that other language. The page felt soft to the touch, much older than all the rest. Next to a few symbols was the word *Hildeleoma*. Then, an intricate drawing of twisting vines and runes. Lana recognized the image immediately. It was one her mother had tattooed down her arm. Lana groaned and tossed the paper alongside the rest. Tattoo plans weren't helpful.

Lana sorted through the books next. All of them were written in that same language. Pressing a hand to her forehead, she scrubbed at her eyebrows. How had she not known something about her mother that was obviously such a big part of her life? What else did Lana not know? She set the books aside and pulled the drawers out of the desk. Her mother had always loved trinkets and the desk was full of them — rocks, crystals, a compass, a beautiful ceremonial dagger, candles, enormous gaudy amulets and rings. Nothing of note. Nothing that revealed anything about that night.

Pushing the chair out of the way, Lana dropped to the floor. She needed to find something, anything, that would explain why her mother would leave her. Lana dumped the contents of the drawers onto the floor in front of her. The jewelry clattered together and thudded heavily against the carpet. But there was nothing.

She wracked her brain. What had her mother said that night?

Don't go outside, especially past the fence, at night. Don't stand in the deep shadows. Avoid the in-between times—all in-betweens lead to Faerie ... tell Lana that I love her. Tell her to look from the dark place.

What did she mean, in-betweens? and looking past the dark? Lana fidgeted with a bracelet at the top of the pile and stared at the space underneath the desk. In-between, like between two things? like a sandwich? She scrunched up her face and instinctively crawled beneath the desk, something she used to do as a small child. The dark beneath her mother's desk had been a safe place for her. Now, as she crouched with her head scrubbing the underside of the desk and her shoulders bumping into the wood, Lana couldn't make sense of her mother's words.

Staring out from beneath the desk, Lana noticed a shock of blue beneath her mother's bed, just barely sticking out. She crawled toward the curious object, which was wedged between the wooden slats beneath the bed. Lana grabbed onto the object and wriggled it from it's hiding place. It was a blue notebook. Lana sat back on her heels and stared at the journal in her hands. *Look from the dark place.* Of course! that's what Lana had called her safe spot beneath the desk as a child. It was the dark place. Her mother wanted her to have this. Wanted her to see this.

Her fingers trembled as she turned the first page, where her mother's handwriting scrawled a letter addressed to her.

My Sweet Little Lana,

I'm sorry. I know it may have been upsetting to hear that I'd gone, but I want you to know that I love you and I'll be back as soon as I can. Do you remember when I told you about the place our family used to live? I have a friend who lives there, and something horrible has happened to her. And it's partially my fault. When your Dad and I left Haven, we did some things that weren't so good. It made things worse for my friend and her family. I can help. She needs me, so I have to go back.

I wish I could have taken you with me, but I can't yet. It's too dangerous there for you right now. I have so much I want to tell you, so much I want to show you.

It may sound strange, but please trust me. When it's night, stay inside with the lights on. If you must go outside, don't go past the fenceline. Avoid the shadows, especially the darkest ones in the forest. More than anything, avoid the in-between times. Dusk is the most dangerous. There are strange things in the world. Things that would hurt you. Please stay safe. If I could do things over again, I would do it differently, but I cannot, so I must fix what I helped worsen.

Don't follow me. I'll be home as soon as I can.

I already miss you.

— Mom

Lana crushed the book against her chest. Her mother hadn't abandoned her without a word. She'd left a letter for her. Just for her. Lana squeezed her eyes shut, but despite her efforts to hold off her tears, they trickled down her cheeks steadily. She shuddered against a sob, wishing she'd burst into the room that night and forced her mother to take her. She should have followed through the portal. No matter what her mother said, she wasn't a kid anymore. She didn't need protecting. At least, not like this. Not by leaving her in a prison of her own fear.

Heat rose in Lana's chest. Her mother was wrong. It wasn't safer here. She would be better off at her mother's side. With renewed vigor, Lana combed through the books again, trying to pull some kind of meaning from any of it, certain there was a way to follow her mother to … Lana looked up at the big window. The morning light had faded to early afternoon. Where had her mother gone? Her mother's words rose unbidden to her mind. *All in-betweens lead to Faerie.* Faerie? Lana blinked heavily.

No. That couldn't be what she meant. That wasn't real.

Just like the living shadows weren't real.

Just like the portal wasn't real.

Lana pushed herself to her feet. She knew what she had seen, so that only meant one thing — her mother had stepped into a portal to the faerie realm. And Lana was now certain of one other thing: she needed to find a portal to Faerie for herself too.

When she saw the shadows behind the diner, the red eyes, there had been something there — a portal. Confronting the shadows might be her only way to find her mother.

So, tonight, she would confront the shadows. Despite the racing of her heart and trembling fingers, Lana settled in to wait for dusk. The time between day and night, where she hoped to get the answers her mother never gave her.

CHAPTER 6

Vasileios — 25 Years Ago in Kaelum

Weeks passed in a blur as Vas studied, meeting with Athan in the mornings and spending most of his afternoons in the library, reading whatever his mentor suggested or brought for him. Taking the long way to the library, he looked out onto the gardens as the afternoon sun stretched across the roses.

He wished he'd started studying magic sooner. Though, he knew his wishing didn't matter. Before the Hollows appeared, he was trapped in hour after hour of what his mother called princely studies—swordsmanship, etiquette, history, and whatever else she deemed important. But with the war, she, and everyone else in the palace, had been much too busy to bother micromanaging his time. He grimaced, trying not to be grateful for the devastation those monsters brought, but it was difficult when, for the first time in his life, he felt alive and free.

His gaze caught on the garden beyond the large windows and he paused, watching the breeze gently stir the grass. A contented exhale caught in his throat when he heard the familiar clacking of heels down the marble hall.

Vas turned, eyes wide, to find his mother standing in front of the enormous doors of the library.

Her eyes softened with relief as she saw him. "Vasileios," she said. "We need to talk."

When she used that tone of voice, he knew something was wrong. He hoped she hadn't found out about his lessons with Athan. His eyes darted back and forth, looking for a means of an escape, despite knowing he couldn't and shouldn't run from his mother. He hadn't run from her since he was still a teenager. Undignified for the prince, she had said. He couldn't get the smell of horse manure out of his boots for at least a week after she'd forced him to work in the stables as punishment.

His mother straightened, crossing her arms with a stern look.

Vas dropped his gaze, repentantly, and focused on her elaborately embroidered skirts instead of her face. "Yes, Mother."

"Now, come along. Your father is waiting for us in the sitting rooms." She led him inside the library through twists and turns. The smell of ink and old leather comforted him despite the situation at hand. At the back of the library, the shelves got tighter and in one corner, a small door hid in the shadows. She gestured for Vas to enter the room, and, hesitantly, he obliged.

The room was small, furnished with a few round tea tables and wooden chairs. His father paced thoughtfully across the room, and a servant, a fae man only a few years older than Vas with long black hair tied neatly at his nape and russet-brown skin, stood in the corner with his head bowed, holding the king's cloak. His father had a habit of tripping on the fabric, or catching it on tables, doors...anything with a corner to be caught on. Vas often wondered why he didn't just abandon the cloak altogether.

"Theo," his mother said, effectively halting the man in his tracks.

He turned with a warm smile. "My love!" The king took two long strides to his wife and gathered her hand in his. "You didn't mention earlier. To what do I owe the pleasure of this lovely meeting?"

She squeezed his hand, bringing it up to her lips for a brief kiss.

Vas looked away. Though he disliked having to witness his parents' affection, it was comforting. He'd heard their love story a hundred times—an unlikely romance in the middle of his mother's Crown Trials.

Though, they were soul mates—a fated love that bound souls together for eternity with golden threads. Soul mates weren't uncommon in Faerie, but still not a guarantee. Even if someone found their mate, bonds could frazzle and break, rejection could snip the fragile threads, but time and trust built that bond into a sturdy rope, like the cord he was certain existed between his parents.

Vas hoped to find his soul mate one day, but he kept that hope quiet and furtive. No one could ever love him, so he shouldn't dare to dream.

"Our upcoming plans," she said.

"Ah, right." His father pulled a chair out from the nearest table for his mother. He held the chair, waiting for her to sit before he sat himself down, gesturing for Vas to join them.

His mother turned to look at the fae in the corner of the room, who still held the cloak with his head bowed so that his long dark hair shadowed his face. "Luze," she said. "You are dismissed."

With a nod, the servant draped the cloak over a chair and left the room.

"He's much quieter than his brother." The king laughed, thanking the man as he left.

Though they had practically grown up together after his father had decided to take the orphaned brothers into the household, Vas had never been close to Luze. Sometimes, he wished things had been different. He watched Luze leave, wondering what it would have been like to have a brother. When the door clicked shut, Vas sat down next to his father, banishing his strange thoughts.

"Vas." His mother hesitated for a moment as she clasped and unclasped her hands on the table. "I know that you have always preferred books to the company of others."

Vas nodded, uncertain where she was going with this.

"Curiosity is an admirable trait," his father added. "Natural, even, for a Brynian."

"But that's the problem," his mother said a bit too quickly. She pressed a finger to her brow and sighed. "It's not natural for Silvids. You cannot rule Silvis as a Brynian. You must rule as a Silvid."

"And how am I supposed to do that?" His voice was weak. "I look nothing like the Silvids. No matter what I do, they'll never accept me. I'm a monster."

His father grasped his shoulder and squeezed. "Vasileios. You are not a monster. They'll accept you. We will find a way. We have plenty of time before you'll ever be expected to rule."

Vas nodded. His parents were still young, only in their late sixties. They would have at least another century before they might consider stepping down for him. Even a century would be early for them to abdicate the throne. *Plenty of time.* The words felt like a weight. *Years. Decades. How long would he spend as the unwanted prince to his people?*

"I may have a solution," his mother said.

Vas looked at her expectantly.

"Marriage," she said.

"Marriage?" Vas looked between his father and mother with furrowed brows.

She nodded. "In the same way the people accept your father, they can accept you. We just need to find you the perfect Silvid bride."

Vas shook his head in disbelief. "An arranged marriage?"

"Of sorts." She clasped her hands delicately in her lap. "You could debut this season. There are many young ladies in the court who could be suitable, with the proper training."

Vas stared, speechless. *Could he accept being the prince of a kingdom who tolerated him only on his wife's behalf?* His eyes drifted to his father, who had married his mother for love—the third son of the Brynian king would have no duty to uphold, no kingdom to run. Vas had never hoped for true love, but the thought of losing even the possibility now struck him like a dagger in the chest.

His mother's voice brought him from his thoughts. "You would have the choice," she said. "You wouldn't need to choose quickly, just wisely."

"There must be some other way." Vas looked to his father for answers. "Some way for me to prove myself to them."

His father stroked his beard, frowning against his hand. "I have no solutions, my son. Your mother and I have been considering this for some time. We want you to be happy among your people—our people. I will continue looking for some other way, but for now, we believe this to be the best way. The safest way."

"The first palace ball of the season is tonight, Vas," his mother added.

"I'll find some other way. I'll—" His thoughts churned. He clenched his fists, digging his nails into his palms with frustration. "I could join the war against the Hollows. I could show them I can protect them."

His mother shook her head, a sorrowful look in her eyes. "I won't let my only son fight in a war against those creatures. We have no idea how many there are or what they are truly capable of. I can't lose you."

Her voice trembled with those last four words in a way that made Vas's throat grow tight.

"If you don't find a suitable bride this season, there will be others, Vas. Perhaps, you'll even fall in love." He grinned. "All we are asking is that you finally join society, my son. In the meantime, I'll speak with my advisors. Athan has always been a genius with issues of public opinion. He got us through the backlash after our marriage." His father smoothed a hand over the front of his clothes.

"Yes," his mother agreed. "You don't need to fight. In that, at least, please, Vasileios, heed me."

Vas bowed his head. "Yes, Mother." His heart was heavy. He would find his own way, even if that meant disobeying his mother again.

The hours before the ball passed far too quickly for Vas. Soon, he was dressed in elaborate clothes and a new cloak with golden embroidery around the hood. His father met him in the hallway and led him to a back entrance to the ballroom.

"Thank you for coming, Vasil." His father gave him a bright, familiar smile. His father's constant joy was a comfort, especially now when his nerves tore into him, making his stomach vibrate with anxiety.

"It's not like I had much choice," he said, with a meaningful look at his mother, who hovered by the door in her fluffy gown with her crown gleaming on her brow, waiting for the perfect moment to make their entrance.

His mother turned to Vas with a nervous smile. "I do wish you wouldn't insist on the cloak, but at least keep it away from your face, dear." She pushed his hood away from his forehead and slipped a thin crown under the fabric to rest atop his head. "Just in case you change your mind."

"Yes, Mother." He never wore the crown, would never show his horns in public, so it didn't matter whether he wore it or not, but he wouldn't begrudge his mother for her request.

Placated by his words, his mother nodded to the servant by the door. Trumpets blared into the ballroom.

"Presenting Queen Harmoni and King Consort Theoden," shouted a servant, while two more pulled the grand doors open for his parents to step into the ballroom. Applause accompanied their entrance.

They made their way through the crowd to the other side, where their two elegant thrones sat. His mother beamed at the crowd and gestured with a regal, gloved hand to where Vas waited just beyond the shadow of the doors.

"And with much delight, I would like to present the Crown Prince Vasileios."

Vas took a deep breath as he stepped into the room to shocked silence. A few of the nobles recovered from the surprise of the season and began to clap; soon, the noise became a roar. Vas wished he could turn around and leave, but the doors swung shut behind him, trapping him in the ballroom with the applause of leering nobility.

"Let us begin the season!" his mother cried.

Music swelled. Fae, in brilliantly colored gowns, twirled around the room, soon oblivious to Vas's presence.

Glad his mother hadn't decided he needed a guard, considering the palace was crawling with them these days, Vas slipped into the crowd and found a shadowed nook to stand in, safe from the laughter of the court that would surely come if he tried to mingle with them. Leaning against a cold marble pillar, he watched the crowd. His mother wanted him to find a Silvid girl to love, to marry, to be the face of the throne when it was his turn to lead, but the thought left a heavy lump in his stomach. A noble Silvid worthy of his mother's crown would never love him.

The music shifted and dances changed. Vas recognized the movements, the songs, though he'd never danced with anyone other than his tutors.

"Would you like to dance?" said a woman to his side.

Vas startled, turning to see the source of the quiet voice. The woman stood at the edge of the shadows. She wore her blonde hair in intricate braids piled high on her head. She smiled hesitantly. Her hands twisted in her deep-red skirts, catching on the lace emblazoned with tiny golden suns. At the sight of the red and gold, his eyes jumped to her ears, round and human. She was from Haven.

When her golden eyes met his bright green, a stillness settled over him, as if the music had slowed and blurred in his mind. He stepped forward without thinking, drawn to her.

"I know it may seem strange, but you just seemed so..." She held out her hand. "You were watching the others so intently, I thought perhaps you might like to...dance."

Vas struggled to find words in the jumble of his thoughts, but slid his palm against hers. The heat of her fingers, twining with his, seeped into his skin, digging deep and soothing some restless part of his soul he hadn't known existed.

"I'm Anastasia," she whispered, drawing closer to him.

Vas felt he should recognize her name, but the reason eluded him. *Anastasia.*

"My name is Vasileios." He waited for her to yank back her hand, but she didn't.

A flash of confusion moved across her face, but Anastasia didn't pull away. "It's so lonely, on the edges of the excitement, but I must admit that I'm not a very good dancer. My father is more interested in training me for wars, rather than dances."

Wars? What war could the humans possibly be training for, Vas thought, but he didn't understand human customs—another side effect of being stuck in the palace his entire life.

"I can dance, in theory. I've been taught to dance, I mean. I could...be your teacher—just for the night. Maybe?" he found himself saying, a smile on his lips, despite the embarrassed heat that suddenly rushed to his cheeks.

Her pale cheeks, dotted with faint freckles, reddened with a blush as she nodded, tightening her hand in his.

Vas pulled her toward him and placed a hand lightly on her waist, while hers rested on his shoulder. His heart thumped loudly in his ears as they moved slowly to the music. Their bodies barely touched as he led her through the dance.

They talked about everything and nothing at all — Haven, the forest surrounding the Palace, the beauty of the stars in the darkest hours of night, her days full of training and his full of study. Time slipped past entirely unheaded while she stood in his arms. Vas surprised himself. He'd never been comfortable in social situations, but talking with her was easier than breathing. He told her things he probably shouldn't have, confessed truths about himself and magic that he never thought he would or could. Perhaps confiding in Athan had made him reckless, but he couldn't help himself. He wanted Anastasia to know everything about him and he wanted to know everything in return.

He hung on her every smile. His heart leapt with each delightful laugh that fell from her lips.

He couldn't pull his gaze away from hers. Caught in the fires of her eyes, they danced until time ceased altogether. No one else existed—only her.

"Vasileios," she was breathless, and her voice carried a note of worry, "my father is walking toward us."

She disentangled herself from him. The loss of her warmth left him feeling empty, already wishing for another moment beside her.

"Anastasia," a stern voice said from behind Vas.

Vas turned, immediately recognizing the face of the Havenite behind him. Commander Creon—the closest thing to a king that Haven had.

Vas bowed his head, respectfully. "Commander Creon, I am pleased to see you at court." His words felt empty as they fell from his mouth, platitudes engrained in him by years of etiquette tutors.

The commander turned his attention from his daughter and gave a curt nod. "Good evening, Prince Vasileios. I would like a word with my daughter, if you'll excuse us."

Vas stepped away, gesturing to Anastasia. "As you desire, Commander." Before her father could drag her away, Vas smiled, catching her eyes one last time. "Thank you for dancing with me. Perhaps I'll find you again on the dance floor."

Creon huffed. "I doubt that, my prince. It seems your mother is looking for you." He gestured into the crowd, where, sure enough, his mother was making her way to him with a small party of Silvid nobles in tow.

Wonderful.

When Vas turned back to Creon, the man was gone, pulling his daughter through the crowd. Vas sighed. Feeling defeated, he walked back to the edge of the room and found another alcove to rest in. If his mother wanted him to meet nobility, then they could all come to him.

Couches lined the walls of the nook, so Vas took advantage of them. He sat, sinking into the cushions to wait on his mother's approach.

She made quick work of the room and soon, his little hiding space was full of people—his mother and three other women.

"My son," his mother said with a happy sigh. "I'd like to introduce you to some wonderful young ladies."

Vas pushed himself from the couch to stand before his mother and her company.

"This is Lady Maia and her daughter, Lady Meredith," she said with a polite flourish of her gloved hand.

Lady Maia, an older fae with silver streaks through her black hair, curtseyed, spreading her dark skirts. Gems were sown into the neckline and dotted the dress like stars.

Meredith mimicked her mother, curtseying with the side of her blue gown delicately held in her hands. Unlike her mother, Meredith's black hair was in a neat bob that ended just at her chin. Her gown was not full of the fluff most women wore, but hung loosely on her thin figure, only gathered at her hips in folds to give the gown shape.

"And this is General Xander's daughter, Alixandra."

"Alix," Meredith corrected as Alix sharply dipped into a curtsey that made the swirling metal that laid over her red dress clink together musically. Alix was tall and muscular and kept her ash-blonde hair pulled tight in a ponytail. Vas wasn't surprised that the general's daughter showed up in a dress that doubled as armor. She seemed like the type to keep a sword hidden down her back as well.

Vas returned the politesse with a bow. "A pleasure to meet you."

"Lady Maia is the matriarch of House Kaesy," his mother said meaningfully. Kaesy was the only duchy in Silvis, meaning Lady Maia was the Duchess of Kaesy and well-respected throughout Silvis...obviously her daughter would be a good marriage prospect. Vas suppressed a grimace at the whole performative affair his mother was imposing on him. His mother laced her fingers with Lady Maia's. "Let's give the children a chance to talk, shall we? I haven't eaten in hours."

The duchess bowed away, and the two older women chattered and laughed on their way to the feast laid out at the far end of the room.

Alix plopped down on the couch as soon as the two women turned away, holding a hand out for Meredith. She took Alix's hand and was immediately pulled down, nearly falling into her lap. Meredith squealed and swatted at Alix, who simply laughed, her eyes glinting with warmth. She held tight to Meredith's hand, turning her gaze to him. Her warm smile twisted into a possessive smirk.

Vas merely rolled his eyes. *What an unpleasant woman.* She was clearly trying to stake her claim to Meredith, but it wasn't like Vas wanted to marry a random noble his mother dumped in front of him. He took a deep breath, barely keeping himself from walking off and leaving them both in the corner alone.

Meredith pulled her hand from Alix's and smoothed her skirts as she situated herself in a more lady-like manner on the couch.

"Prince," Meredith began. "I realize why my mother presented me to you, and I feel as if you and I can work through some kind of understanding."

Despite Alix's eyes boring into him, Vas sat down. "Okay?"

"Do you want to be married?" Meredith asked.

"Well…" Vas said. "Not like this. No. I want to marry for love, and that will never happen."

"Exactly," she said. "But we could help each other." Meredith's fingers intertwined with Alix's again. "I am completely, wholly, uninterested in marrying you."

Her words stung, but Vas already knew that no one would want to marry him, especially not someone so clearly already in love.

Meredith continued. "And it's not as if my mother will let me marry a mere soldier like Alix." Alix stiffened beside her, jaw clenching. "If my marriage to you falls through, she'll find another young noble for me to marry who will better our standing or provide some gain to the house."

"Where do I fall in all of this?" Vas crossed his arms tight against his chest. Alix's stare made him quite uncomfortable.

"Well, that depends." Her fingers squeezed tighter on Alix's until Vas could see the white on her knuckles. "I feel as if I can trust you, so I'll ask…what do you want from life? What is your greatest desire?"

"That seems like a big question." He knew what he wanted. He wanted to be normal, to be a king the Silvids would love and accept. But, instead of telling Meredith all that, his eyes searched the crowd and landed on Anastasia.

"Of course it is, silly prince, but I think I know what you want. I've heard the rumors." She leaned across the couches toward him, lowering her voice. "You can shift, can't you? So it only makes sense that you'd want magic returned to Silvis, right? You are Brynian, after all—descendant of the Wild Court, where magic flows freely. It makes sense that you'd wish for a taste of your father's homeland."

His eyes widened, gaze darting around. "What? No." *Had she heard something? What did she know?* He wiped his sweaty palms against his trousers. *What rumors had she heard?*

Meredith shushed him. "There's no one else around. Be honest. Wouldn't it be better if we had magic? If the Silvids accepted their true nature, we would be as we were meant to be. Don't you want that?"

Vas's thoughts flitted back to that ruined page he'd read not long ago. Magic had once existed in Silvis, but she couldn't be right, could she? Her words repeated in his mind—*as we were meant to be.*

"Wait." Alix's possessive glare finally fell away as she looked to Meredith with wide, confused eyes. "You said nothing about magic to me."

Meredith patted Alix on the thigh. "Magic is in our nature, just like it is in yours, prince. You and I could usher in a new era."

"Meredith." Alix's voice wavered, sounding nervous and hurt.

"That's not possible." Vas shook his head.

"It will be slow going, yes, but—" Meredith tucked a strand of hair behind her ear. She caught his eyes, a pleading passion written in the lines of her face. "With your help, I believe it's possible."

"I don't know." He sunk back into the couch, putting distance between himself and the two strange fae before him. He'd never even considered the possibility. What would Silvis be like if the fae accepted magic? How could they even bring it about? He wanted to trust her. He wanted to believe, but the Silvids were full of fear. Fear breeds hate, the enemy of acceptance. It wouldn't work. He shook his head.

"Just think about it," she said. "We live in Haven with the humans. At the very least, it would be an excuse to see Anastasia. I saw you dancing with her earlier. Your mother would never let you marry a human, you know, but if you were to marry me, you could be with anyone you pleased." Meredith stood and pulled Alix up with her. The two walked away with angry whispers bouncing between them.

Meredith was right, at least in one thing: she might be his only shot at a relationship with Anastasia. He dropped his face into his hands, wishing he could force the Silvids to accept him and whoever he chose as queen—fae or not.

CHAPTER 7

Vasileios — 25 Years Ago in Kaelum

For the first time in over a month, Vas spent his morning alone. He frowned at the book splayed across his lap, his mind not quieting. He wanted to practice, but Athan was in a war meeting—not to mention the weather had turned stormy. The cloud cover was so complete it was nearly dark as night, and even Athan was cautious when it came to darkness. *The Hollows might appear*, he'd said, echoing sentiments across the entire palace. They were just paranoid. Hollows hadn't been seen this far inland. The capital was safe.

Vas tilted his head back against the cushion of his favorite library chair, trying to chase away his thoughts. His fingers itched for the feel of magic sparking across his skin. He looked around, scanning the library. Guards stood at the entrances; even the ancient librarian—the caretaker of the books—seemed on high alert. He scoffed underneath his breath. *Did they all think the Hollows would just burst through the windows and devour us all? Ridiculous.*

He stood and slipped through the stacks, making his way to the darkest corner. When he was certain no one would notice, he shifted into the smallest, but quickest form he knew—a mouse. He laughed at his own cleverness. Every day, he snuck out through the holes in the wall that no one noticed, and today was just like any other day.

He scurried outside, despite the mud and drizzle, running as quickly as he could to that secret place. He hopped through the bars in the secret door that Athan had shown him and only shifted back into his fae form when he was safe in the practice clearing. This was the first time he'd come here by himself.

Despite the gloomy weather, he smiled, shaking the rain from his drenched hair. He leaned back against one of the thick trees, taking shelter from the light rain. He slid down, relaxing against the cragged tree trunk. Cradled by roots that jutted from the ground, Vas focused on the magic of the world around him. He could feel the pulse of the tree beneath him, and he pulled gently, connecting that magical heartbeat to his own.

Fueled by the forest's energy, he muttered, "*Genip*," and a purple fog swirled slowly in the palm of his hand.

He wanted to try something big, something more difficult. Athan had only been teaching him the basics, walking him through the theories, a few simple spells, like the fog spell, and forcing him to practice pulling magic to fuel his spell from the air around him over and over again. But mostly, he'd just taught him defensive spells—counter spells and wardings. It reminded him of how his mother had only let him learn shifting as a means of escape. He wanted something more. It had taken him weeks of begging for Athan to help him learn the concealment spell.

With that thought, Vas decided to practice. Currently, the concealment spell was his best hope for hiding his horns. A hand mirror, from yesterday's lesson on observation spells leaned against a nearby tree. Vas scooted over, peering into the glass until his face was visible.

"*Behydan.*" He twisted his fingers across his horns. The air around his head shimmered with deep-purple smoke before sinking down and wrapping around his horns. Vas stared intently, the steady rain pattering along with his hopeful heart. He hadn't tried this yet. He was too embarrassed to try in front of Athan.

Inch by inch, his horns disappeared—or at least, mostly. When he twisted his head, the dim light cast the shadow of his horns and there was a faint glimmer to the air where they should be.

Vas sighed. His mother would certainly notice the magic glimmer. The courtiers would notice. The illusion was useless. He needed a permanent solution. *Though, could he even convince his parents that his horns were gone? Would they believe they just fell off one day?* He laughed wryly at the thought. *Useless.*

His shoulders slumped. Did he have to hide everything about himself? His horns, his magic...even his interest in a Havenite would be distasteful. From his father's stories, the court had a hard enough time accepting a Brynian as the queen's consort, but a human would be another thing entirely. If only the court could see, could understand, how beautiful magic could be, maybe that would be enough for him—for them to accept even one part of him.

Vas widened his arms suddenly, whispering words into the air as purple light filled the space between his hands.

"*Cyme heofan,*" he said. The air spun in his hands, shimmering with magic, until it slowed, revealing a beautiful night sky of twinkling stars. Vas watched the illusory clouds move lazily across the stars between his hands. If he could show the court this, what would they do? The court wouldn't appreciate magic's beauty. They would surely clamor for him to be cast out, thrown into the desert with the other beasts.

Vas pushed his hands together, forcing the sky to collapse upon itself. More complex spells, like the magic mirror spell, required layering spells together—a difficult task, but difficult was exactly what Vas wanted. He wanted a challenge.

He pulled on the magic of the forest again, drawing in energy as easily as drawing a breath. "*Beseo woruldlic.*" He struggled to maintain the spell before shoving it toward the hand mirror still reclining on the nearby tree. Sweat formed on his brow as the image finally took shape, flickers of another world. He watched as humans walked on pale stone paths, lining the fronts of tall, shining buildings of glass.

The image shook, faltering, and Vas exhaled, letting the magic fall away. Feeling proud of his progress, Vas planned to ask Athan to tell him how to conjure images of other worlds besides just the mundane world. He wanted to see the other fae realms beyond Kaelum.

He stretched, standing with the support of the tree. He looked up at the sky. The rain had stopped, but it was still dark, like dusk had descended upon the forest early. He furrowed his brows, only now realizing he'd spent much longer than he'd realized beyond the castle walls. Reddish pink streaked at the distant horizon, and stars dappled the sky where the clouds began to part. It truly was dusk.

Vas took a deep breath, readying himself to head back to the palace, but a strange scent made him pause. Rot floated on the breeze. Grimacing, Vas searched the shadows of the surrounding trees. Two pinpoints of glowing red peered from the dark depths of the forest.

The dots grew larger, closer. *Eyes.* Vas took a careful step away. His heart raced. Those eyes were shoulder height to Vas's six feet. The smell of rotting flesh overwhelmed him as the creature approached with heavy footfalls crunching on the scattered branches and undergrowth.

Conscious of each movement and sound he made, Vas took careful steps toward the edge of the clearing. The creature's eyes followed his movements. It was close now. Its breath came in and out in a snuffling sound, as if it were sniffing the air.

Vas stumbled away, bumping into the trees. Those jerky movements were enough to excite the reeking beast. It bounded into the clearing, giving Vas a clear view of it for the first time.

A Hollow. The glare of red eyes locked onto Vas, and adrenaline shot through him. He was face-to-face with a Hollow.

The wolf-like beast was at least twice the size of a normal wolf, with heavy clawed paws and a narrow muzzle full of sharp teeth. Gashes in its dark flesh revealed black, rotting wounds and exposed bones. Red, fleshy vines wrapped around its throat and front legs, sparking with light. Those same red vines stitched between the wounds, holding the beast together.

Vas froze. His thoughts raced with all the things he'd ever learned about the creatures. Hollows consumed magic and hated the sun. They were the ultimate predator of the fae, and here Vas was playing with magic as twilight set in. It shouldn't be here. They were supposed to be safe from the Hollows here. Hollows only lived in the desert. *Didn't they?*

The Hollow opened its massive jaws, revealing rows of jagged teeth, and howled—a horrible screeching howl, as if the creature's vocal cords were made of grinding rocks. The death knell reverberated in Vas's ears. He turned and ran. If he could get through the door and back into the palace walls, he would be safe. His thoughts scrambled. *Faster. Faster.*

Breath rasped in Vas's throat as he ran, pushing his body as hard as he could to outrun the monster bounding behind him. He didn't even feel as thorns from the underbrush snagged against his legs, leaving blood trails on his flesh. On two legs, he was no match for its speed, but the door was so close. He threw himself into a shift, willing himself to be even faster. His body shrank into a sparrow and he took flight, barely dodging the snapping jaws of the Hollow.

The Hollow was gaining on him. Vas threw himself at the iron grates, shifting in the air again. As a mouse, he easily slipped through the thin bars and hit the ground rolling on the other side. The Hollow collided with the locked door, metal groaning against stone.

The creature's claws raked against the door, rattling on its hinges. The Hollow growled, sending Vas's blood pulsing in his veins. He shifted back to his natural form and scrambled away, putting distance between himself and the beast gnawing at the iron. Its red eyes flitted wildly as spit frothed at its gaping maw.

Vas had escaped. Just barely, but he was safe in the palace garden. The fear that had been winding tight in his chest released and a hysterical laugh bubbled out of Vas. But his relief lasted only a moment as the hinges squealed in protest before snapping completely beneath the Hollow's weight.

It was inside the courtyard walls. Vas swiveled where he stood and ran, putting as much distance between himself and the creature as it struggled through the narrow doorway. *It was in the palace. He had brought the creature into his home. His parents.* Vas slid to a stop.

He led this monster straight to his parents' doorstep. *How had it even gotten into the forest?* The capital was supposed to be safe. His first instinct was to run, but he couldn't. He wouldn't. Vas steeled himself.

The courtyard sat empty for now, though Vas could see guards gathering in the distance, close to the palace entrance. The beauty of the garden stood in contrast to the disgusting creature entering the courtyard. Bells rang, alerting everyone of danger inside the walls of the palace.

Though his hands shook, Vas ran toward the beast, ignoring the screams of fae in the distance. The smell of roses and the Hollow's rot mixed together nauseatingly.

Vas's heart thrummed with terror as he neared the gnashing teeth. His body rippled as he shifted into an enormous panther. In the instant his muscled paws slammed into the side of the beast, he wished he could wield the magic of the Silvids and open the earth to swallow the Hollow whole in one fell swoop. The creature shuddered under his blow, but didn't move.

Vas and the Hollow struggled against each other, scratching and tearing. A scream was wrenched from Vas's throat as the Hollow landed a blow on his shoulder, ripping open his flesh. Bright-red blood dropped to the ground and soaked into Vas's black fur.

Despite the alarm bells still ringing across the garden, Vas focused, forcing all his will into the thought—*Geefenlaecan.* Vas's magic exploded from his body in a wave of purple smoke. When the magic cleared, three bloody panthers now circled the growling Hollow. Despite his fear, a flicker of pride welled in Vas's heart. His duplication illusion worked perfectly. His secret lessons were paying off.

The nightmare of living decay jerked its head, dripping putrid black blood as it took in the three panthers. Vas and his doppelgangers swiped in unison, but the creature dodged easily, ducking and rolling away from his paws. Vas couldn't hold the illusion for long, but perhaps it would be long enough to get the upper hand.

The Hollow tracked his movements, shifting its gaze between the illusions and the reality. It took all of Vas's spare attention to maintain the spell, so he couldn't control his illusions independently yet. This had to be enough.

He circled around the beast, grass soft beneath his paws. Vas stopped near the Hollow's back—the two fake panthers in front—before he and his illusions lunged, mouth open, fangs bared. The Hollow danced away from the illusions, snapping at one of the doppelgangers. Its teeth slid through air, finding no purchase in the fake panther.

Vas struck in that moment of confusion. Vas's fangs sank into the rotting flesh of the Hollow's back. Bile rose in his throat as the black blood ran down his jaws and touched his tongue. The Hollow jerked, throwing its head back, as it struggled to toss Vas off, but he held on. Its flesh ripped, thick blood flowing freely from the beast.

The Hollow howled, the sound barely audible over the alarm bells. It stood up on its back paws, then threw itself backward onto the ground, crashing its weight down on Vas, their bodies crushing a bed of pansies. Pain rattled through his body as his head smacked into the cold, firm dirt. His jaws opened, releasing the Hollow as he gasped for air and the illusory panthers faded away.

The creature crawled from Vas's limp form, its claws digging into his flesh and opening bloody wounds across his stomach. Vas struggled to push himself to his feet, his muscles trembling.

The Hollow crouched by the rose garden fence, readying for its next attack, despite the gore that pooled at its feet. Their bodies crashed together again. Over and over again. The beast was stronger. He couldn't withstand another punishing blow. They stared at each other. The only end to this would be death—his own.

When it finally lunged, he knew he would be too slow to move. Vas readied himself to take the brunt of the blow. He would accept death at this beast's claws.

But beneath the creature's dog-like paws, the ground shifted, twisted unnaturally, and the creature tripped. It stumbled and fell with a heavy thud onto a thick stake of fencing that surrounded his mother's favorite yellow roses. The gurgle of rotten flesh sinking down on wood sent a wave of nausea through Vas. The creature flailed, desperate to escape, but its frenzy only hastened its demise. The Hollow rattled out a final breath and went still. Its blood and entrails leaked across the path in a river of gore that made Vas shudder as bile rose in his throat.

The way the ground moved—had that been Silvid magic? *Had he somehow used it without knowing? Had someone else?* Vas looked up from the corpse.

The bells finally faded. In the silence of the slain beast, Vas realized the courtyard was no longer empty. Members of the court watched from the high balconies of the palace. A terrified hush covered the scene.

His mother stood, trembling at the edge of the rose garden, his father holding her in his arms. *Had his mother saved him with Silvid magic? Impossible.* He dismissed the thought. She didn't use magic. She wouldn't use magic. Athan stood near his parents in the shadow of a tree, a proud smile in his eyes. *Had it been Athan? Had Athan saved him?*

Head bowed, Vas, still in panther form, walked to his parents' side. His mother remained utterly silent, still trembling as she placed her palm atop Vas's feline head. His father squeezed his wife before pulling away to toss his own cloak over his son's form.

"You're alive," he said quietly. Compassion and fear tinged his father's words. His father draped a hand across Vas's shoulders, then took his mother's hand to lead them both away from the carnage.

As they passed, Athan whispered, "The strength of a king. You did well, Prince."

Vas didn't respond, couldn't respond. He kept his head low so that his father's cloak shadowed his eyes.

His father cleared his throat. "Athan, take care of the mess," he said, as he tightened his grip on Vas and his mother.

Athan bowed in acceptance of the gruesome task.

His father led them through the crowd of nobles who had gathered in the courtyard. The men and women flinched away from Vas, horror evident in their eyes as they watched him—the magic wielder—pass by. Vas kept his head low, hoping none of the court would guess it was him hiding beneath the feline form.

He was used to their sidelong glances of distaste for the prince who refused to take part in court. But if they knew the extent of his abilities, his magic? If they knew he'd been practicing magic here on the palace grounds? What would they do then? He was the only Brynian on the palace grounds other than his father. What would they tell the people? How would they cover this up? They'd all seen him use magic, obviously Brynian magic. They would know and blame him for the Hollow appearing. Maybe it was his fault. Vas's stomach dropped with guilt. *Had the last few months of learning magic brought the Hollow here?*

Finally, in the safety and privacy of the queen and king's chambers, his mother began to sob, throwing her arms around Vas, who still felt numb from the shock of seeing a Hollow for the first time.

"You could have died, you reckless boy. What were you thinking? Why were you out there?" she sobbed, clinging to her son's shoulders.

"Shift," his father said quietly.

His mother gasped as she pulled away, covered in bright-red blood. His blood. "Vasileios. Vasileios," she said, fear making her voice pitch higher.

With a slow exhale, Vas let the change come over him. His body contracted. A shift had never been so painful. The deep gashes in his shoulder and stomach stretched with the shift. The fall had broken a rib. His bones snapped back in place, and he screamed in agony as he returned to his natural form. Through the pain, Vas's thoughts ran in circles.

He crouched on the floor, still covered by his father's cloak. His mother moved to his side and carefully pulled the cloak away, revealing his shredded clothes soaked with blood. His mother's eyes widened, searching him, inspecting every wound visible. His upper arm was cut down to the bone. He hadn't even noticed the gaping hole in his thigh, seeping blood onto the carpet.

She hovered with indecision before she began to move, melting into the stoic mask of the queen of the Silvids.

"Lay down," she commanded, and he did.

Vas lay on the floor in front of her as her hands fluttered over his wounds. Red light sparked and moved like mist across his skin. Vas hissed as his flesh moved on its own accord, knitting together beneath his mother's hands.

His eyes widened in realization as he looked at his mother's face. "Mama..." he whispered.

She shook her head and kept her attention focused on the magic she was working before his eyes—the wordless magic of the Silvids, fueled by the magic in their own souls. The very thing every Silvid was taught to hate out of fear of becoming corrupted or luring hungry monsters to their homes. His mother was breaking her own rules for him. Her once blue eyes were now ringed with vibrant red, a red too close to the red of the Hollow's eyes. The color leached into the blue. The red brightened with each wound she closed.

"I just wanted to protect you. I wanted to show everyone that I will be a good king," Vas murmured, growing more exhausted by the second.

"You certainly showed them something," the king said with a soft chuckle. "That was some impressive magic, which can only mean you've been going against your mother's wishes to practice." The king sounded proud despite the reprimand.

When she finished, Vas was completely healed; not even a bruise remained on his skin. His mother stepped back, wobbling on her feet. His father was quick to sweep in, wrapping his arms around his wife to keep her steady. He whispered softly against her ear. Vas turned his head, clenching his eyes shut against tears that threatened to fall. Vas wondered whether he would ever be ready to take the throne—whether the Silvids would ever accept him.

CHAPTER 8

Vasileios — 25 Years Ago in Kaelum

"Send the mage out!" voices cried from beyond the closed door. "Send it to the desert!"

Vas blinked, looking around the room. He was still in his parents' chambers, but no longer on the floor. Reclining on a bed that he didn't remember being in his parents' sitting room, Vas took stock of his body. He felt fine—a bit tired, but fine. His father and Athan stood by the door at the far end of the room, where a guard stood, holding the door shut against what seemed to be a crowd, pleading for entrance.

"It's been days!" someone shouted. "Send the mage to Haven! Send the mage to fight!"

To fight? They wanted him to fight? Vas hadn't been surprised they wanted to exile him to the desert, but to fight? The words beyond the door settled over him, and Vas jolted up. *Days.* He'd been asleep for days. He ran a hand down his body, then through his hair. Someone had changed his clothes and combed his hair—all while he was comatose. His eyes roamed around the room, landing on Athan and his father.

"Theoden," Athan said. "Perhaps they're right. Did you see what he pulled off while he shifted? I have never even heard of casting illusions while shifted, not to mention—the shift itself. Did you already know?"

Pride glowed in Vas's chest, pleased at his teacher's praises. He hadn't even known casting Brynian magic while shifted was unusual. As long as he used the words as a channel for the magic, it made sense it would work. He shifted on the bed, but they hadn't noticed he was awake yet. Curious what his father might say, Vas remained as still and quiet as he could.

"Of course I knew his shifts were...different, but I cannot allow this." He pointed toward the clamor beyond the door. "Harmoni would have my head if I let our son go to war." Theoden gestured to the guard that stood beside them as he spoke. "Guard. Disperse the courtiers. Use force if necessary."

Shifts were different? Vas furrowed his brows. *What was his father talking about? What did they mean?* Vas ran through everything he'd remembered about their shifting lessons, but nothing came to mind. He was certainly an incredibly quick shifter and talented enough to take on almost any form if he'd seen it before or studied its anatomy. That must be what he meant, Vas decided, though an uneasiness lingered in his stomach.

Athan reached out, placing a hand on the guard's arm as he spoke. "Wait. Theo, think for a moment—if a mage were to solve the Hollow problem, Silvids may see things differently. Even more so if the future king were the one to solve them." Athan's eyes slid to Vas; relief softened his gaze as he noticed Vas was awake. "Would they not be forced to acknowledge, accept even, the one who solved this crisis, magic or no?"

"No," his father said sternly. "Do not speak of absurdity."

"As you desire," Athan said slowly. He lifted his hand from the guard's arm, who immediately slipped out of the room to deal with the courtiers clamoring at the door. "I'll keep watch over the prince, if you wish to check on the queen. Perhaps she has woken from her exhaustion—as the prince has." Athan gestured toward Vas, who offered a halfhearted smile.

"Vasil." His father rushed to his side. "How are you, my son?"

Vas's thoughts spun. *Could the Silvids see him as a hero? Could they accept his magic if he saved them?*

"Vasileios?" his father repeated, leaning to look into his eyes. His brows furrowed with concern. "Are you all right?"

Vas nodded. "Yes," he said, his voice hoarse from disuse. "I'm fine. Is Mother okay? What happened?"

"After healing you, she was just a bit tired, that's all," his father said, though his smile stretched a bit too thin across his lips. He was worried.

"She's still asleep?" Vas anxiously clenched his fists in the soft fabric of the blanket he'd been covered with.

"Well, yes. She just needed extra rest after all the excitement. You don't need to worry. I'll go check on your mother, while you get some more rest." He pushed up from where he'd been kneeling beside Vas.

"I'll come with you." Vas pushed up from the cushions, but pain jolted through his leg where he'd been injured and his heart raced with the effort. The room spun, and Vas sank back down onto the couch.

"I'll just be in the bedroom." His father gestured to a door at the back of the room. "We kept you close by so I could stay with you both. Athan will stay with you, and I'll be right back." His father pressed a gentle hand to his forehead, as if checking for fever. "Just rest, Vasil."

"All right." Vas closed his eyes for a moment as his father left the room to check on his mother. Guilt twisted in his gut. It was his fault his mother was sick and his father was worried. He'd caused this. He'd drawn the Hollow to the palace. He needed to fix this somehow. He needed to do something.

When the door clicked shut behind his father, Vas opened his eyes to stare at his teacher, who sat on the floor at his side.

"Wonderful to see you finally awake, my prince." Athan stretched an arm along the edge of the bed to brace himself as he turned toward Vas.

Alone with his magic teacher, his thoughts returned to what Athan had said before the guard left: *If a mage were to solve the Hollow problem.* "Would the Silvids really accept me? You think I could actually defeat the Hollows?"

Athan's brows raised with surprise and his hand patted a soft rhythm on the mattress. "They would be forced to, I would expect. How could they not love a war hero? Their savior?"

"I couldn't possibly be some hero for the Silvids. You think I could do it?" Vas stared up at the ceiling. He couldn't imagine fighting another Hollow, let alone multiple. He'd barely gotten out of that fight alive. If someone hadn't saved him... "Did you save me? Did you twist the mud beneath the Hollow's foot? "

Athan's lips parted for a moment before snapping shut. "I didn't save you, and neither did the queen. We were much too far away to have done anything. The creature must have slipped," Athan said.

Though Vas didn't believe him, he didn't say as much.

Athan continued speaking. "You have more potential than you realize. I can teach you to rise to your potential."

If Athan believed in him, he could save the Silvids. He could save his parents. If he was could do it, then he had to try. What kind of prince would he be if he just hid from the problems? What kind of son would he be if he didn't at least try to protect his family? "I'll do it," Vas said.

Athan blinked in surprise and leaned closer. "It will be a bit more complicated than just running in and lucking into defeating a creature on its own. The one you killed was weak, half-starved, and alone. The desert is full of Hollows. They are pack hunters with magic of their own. Not to mention, you'll be going directly against your parents' wishes. You do realize this, yes?"

Vas closed his eyes, taking deep breaths to calm his racing heart. "I'll do whatever I must." He would use magic to save the Silvids, then they'd see. Magic wasn't something to be feared, but harnessed.

Athan patted the blanket twice as he stood. "We will be accelerating your lessons. In one week, there will be a convoy heading to Haven. I'll arrange for you to join—in disguise, of course. Just for a day. I think it would be good for you to see the desert for yourself."

Vas's eyes snapped open as he looked to his teacher. "You'll be coming with me, right?"

"I have too many duties here. You'll be surrounded by guards and travel will only be during daylight, so you shouldn't even see any Hollows. If, after traveling the desert, you still want to pursue this path, then I will do everything I can to help you become the savior of Silvis."

"Okay." Vas struggled with excitement and fear. He imagined walking into court as a hero. The courtiers would applaud as he sat on the throne. At last, he would belong.

CHAPTER 9

Lana

The sun sank below the horizon, and twilight slowly descended upon Lana's home. She stood in the front yard, safe behind the fence, waiting for dusk to truly come. In the woods, the shadows deepened and intersected, layering darkness on darkness to create spots of pure night. In those dark spots, Lana felt eyes watching her. She searched the shadows. Nothing. But the weight of a stranger's gaze still settled on Lana's back as she paced along the grass. She'd never been fond of the dark, and it didn't seem to be very fond of her, either.

Marty stepped out onto the front porch. "Li'Lana?" he asked, using the nickname her mother often called her. "You should get inside. It's getting late."

"It's alright. I just need a little air." Lana continued to pace, waiting for something to happen.

Marty entered the house and emerged again only moments later to sit down on his favorite rocking chair. He rocked in the weather-battered chair on the front porch and dropped a longsword with strange letters down the blade and a golden hilt in his lap — a familiar sight in recent years. Before her mother left, the sword hung on the wall in the living room, but now it was Marty's nighttime companion.

Lana asked him once why a sword, but his answer hadn't made sense. "Creatures in the woods," he'd said. If he was worried about bears, it seemed reasonable to have a weapon, but a shotgun would do more than a sword. And the shadow beasts? She doubted a sword would be much of a weapon against them.

Marty's attention never wavered from the woods, from the places where the shadows stretched toward them like greedy hands as the sun sank lower and lower in the sky. The light from the house and the lanterns hanging around the yard.

The sudden ringing of her cellphone broke the silence, and Lana jumped. She scrambled for her phone and answered it.

"Hey, Bestie~!" Liam's voice floated through the phone. Her closest and only friend since childhood. Liam had always been at her side. When her father died, Liam was there. All throughout school. When her mother disappeared. He was the one constant in her life. "I'm on my way with a surprise for you."

For a split second, she relaxed at the sound of his voice, until his words registered. On his way? No. He couldn't. It was nearly dusk. If she was right, if her mother really was in

Faerie, and the monsters from her nightmares were arriving, then Liam couldn't be here. She couldn't survive losing him too.

"What?! No. Why? It's so late. You really shouldn't." The last rays of sunlight glinted in Lana's eyes before sinking beyond the horizon.

"Late? It's barely 7:50. It's like, not even remotely your bedtime. What are you? Ten?" He laughed, but the sound drifted off and he took a more serious tone. "I know today is a rough day for you, so I'm coming to see you. Don't push me away."

What was he talking about? "A rough day?"

Lana could hear him take a deep breath. "With your mom, since today is ... you know."

Oh. Lana blinked up at the darkening sky. Today was the anniversary of her mother's disappearance. The spring equinox. She suddenly felt incredibly stupid for not realizing it sooner — it was another in-between time, wasn't it? The time between seasons.

"Right," she said softly. "But, you really should just go home. We can talk tomorrow. I promise I'm okay."

"It's a bit late for that," he said. Lana fell silent, listening. Headlights swept through the sparse trees at the front of her yard, and the grumbling of a car engine filled the air. It was too late. Liam was already here.

He parked the car by the fenceline and turned it off. His headlights, the blessed beams, stayed on, lighting the grass between the car and the gate. He stared at Marty on the porch with his sword. Lana knew that Liam didn't understand — couldn't understand. All he could see was her crazy stepdad, who never left the property and carried a sword around like a pet.

She rushed to the front gate, shoving her phone in her pocket. The damp grass brushed against her ankles, sending goose bumps along her legs. The evening was entirely silent. Eerily silent. Even the breeze was hushed against the branches.

Sliding out of the car, Liam stepped toward her and lingered in the arch of the fence gate, which had once been covered in blue morning glories, but now held white Christmas lights wrapped around the lattice—no matter the time of year. The light hit his face at several angles, creating spots of bright and dark that were sinister and comforting all at once on his familiar face. Her heart stuttered at his easy smile, unaware of the danger lurking in the night.

Lana ran her hands along her arms to ease the chill that she couldn't dispel. He still stood in the in-between—the place between the fenced-in yard and the darkness beyond. Lana's fingers itched to pull him forward. Her mother's words rang in her head: *Don't go beyond the fence; avoid the shadows and in-betweens.* If she pulled him into the yard, what would he think? Would he think she was insane, paranoid like Marty?

Maybe if she just started walking, he would follow, so Lana took a few steps toward the house. She cast her gaze over her shoulder to see whether he was following.

"Are you okay?" Liam asked, smile faltering, but he didn't move.

Lana's eyes darted to the woods, where the shadows almost seemed to undulate between the trees. "I'm fine. You should hurry home before it gets too late. I'll talk to you tomorrow." Her words tumbled out in a rush.

Liam hesitated, so close to the gate—so close to the darkness. "You seem on edge. If you need somewhere else to stay tonight..." His eyes drifted back to Marty, who kept his silent watch. "You isolate yourself too much. Especially today, but if you really want me to leave, I will, but why not come with me for a little while?"

"I'm just—" Her words stuck in her throat as the headlights clicked off, throwing the yard past the fence into darkness. "What happened to your lights?"

Liam glanced back at the car. "They're automatic." In the absence of the headlights, the darkness thickened behind him. "What is that?" he murmured as the air warbled and shimmered.

"No." Lana clutched the fence, eyes glued to that familiar darkness that haunted every nightmare. He shouldn't be here. She was the only one that should face the shadows, not him. "Liam! Run!" she screamed, but he didn't listen.

He didn't even have time to.

From the glittering darkness emerged a snarling snout of black fur, shadow, and bone. Red eyes soon followed, blinking out of the murky darkness with a hungry violence.

Lana screamed as she stumbled backward, her hands clawing at Liam, but unable to find purchase on his arm to pull him back with her. Marty rushed off the porch, his footsteps a raucous clatter on the wooden steps. He swung the sword as he moved, muttering strange words beneath his breath. With a final word, fire burst from the sword, searing down the blade.

Liam dodged out of the way as the nightmare beast fell to the ground in front of him, having pulled its large, wolfish body from the shadowy portal. He scrambled toward Lana, putting as much distance as he could between the beast and himself.

Lana clutched his hands. Her eyes darted between the portal and the creature. It was the thing of her nightmares—the beasts that reeked of rot and chased her through the desert in her dreams. But the portal? That was her ticket to Faerie. Her entire body trembled. She couldn't do it. All of her bravery crumpled when faced with the monster from her nightmares.

The creature stepped forward, across the fence line, but smoke rose from the its paw, burning with golden sparks of ethereal flame. It stumbled, yanking its foot back over the line. Its clumsy movement gave Marty the perfect opportunity. He twirled the sword with a practiced grace, slicing through the monster's jaw in one smooth motion.

At the touch of flame, the creature howled in pain, screaming its agony to the sky. Fire leapt along its fur, meeting the red sparks that danced along its body. Suddenly and completely engulfed in fire, the wolf-monster fell to the ground and smoldered to ash.

Lana breathed a sigh of relief, but she should have known her terror wasn't over yet. All around the house, shimmering portals opened into an endless darkness. Red eyes lurked and drew closer. *She was supposed to be safe here. The house was safe. Why were they suddenly here?* Lana barely held back a sob.

"Get in the house," Marty barked, brandishing his flaming sword. The creatures slowly surrounded the entire house, but never stepped past the fence.

For a moment, Lana was transfixed by that wavering flame, flickering along the sharp metal. It was somehow familiar. Comforting. She yearned to hold it herself, to slay the creatures and save herself, but she couldn't. She felt ridiculous for even wasting time imagining it.

Liam grabbed her hand and they ran inside, hiding in the hallway—the one place in the house with no windows. She didn't want to see the menacing stares beyond the fence.

Huddled in the lights of the house, Lana could almost pretend they were safe. Almost.

"What is even going on?" Liam muttered, running a frustrated hand through his hair. "Am I hallucinating?"

Lana squeezed his hand. "You're not seeing things."

"How does Marty even know how to use a sword?" Liam's voice lowered to barely above a whisper, as if the creatures outside might hear them talking and somehow manage to jump past the fence. "What happened out there?"

"Mom met him at a fencing club, but the sword is Mom's—a family sword, so…" Lana trailed off. "He must have known this would happen." The night her mother left resurfaced in her mind. "She told him. She told him they'd found a way here. *Nowhere is safe.*" She repeated her mother's words from the last time she'd ever seen her. "The nightmares are real…and Mom…" Lana furrowed her brows, slowly puzzling together her thoughts. *If her mother had gone to stop the creatures from coming here, then did that mean she'd failed? Was her mother dead, wherever she was?* What had really happened? What was truth and what was a well-meaning lie?

"Lana," Liam said, his voice tense and urgent. "We need to get somewhere. We need to leave." He pulled on her hand, dragging her down the hallway.

Lana blinked. In the hallway, despite the lights stretching to every corner, a dark portal was forming, warbling into existence. "No—this can't be." *Hallway.* Lana's heart stuttered in her chest. The hallway was a place between rooms—an in-between. "Hurry! Into the living room!"

Lana jerked Liam alongside her as they ran into the first door they came across. The curtains were open. Nausea welled up Lana's throat at the sight beyond the windows. Red eyes lurked in the darkness beyond the fence, which still stood. From the safety of the lit yard, Marty ran around, shaking the sword at the creatures, daring them to step close enough for him to touch.

The house was completely surrounded with snarling, hungry monsters.

From the hallway, a male voice echoed. "I can't hold this portal for long!" he called. "I know you can see with your own eyes that it's not safe here."

"Who are you?" Liam glared toward the empty doorway. He took a step between Lana and the door, as if expecting someone to rush through and attack.

"Is this really the time for introductions?" the voice said, scoffing. "I'm Shiloh Leigdraca of Haven. If you ever want to be safe again, your only option is to defeat them at the source. In that—I believe we can help each other."

"How can I trust you?" Lana stepped toward the doorway. She wanted to trust him. She wanted to believe that someone could help her, that somehow, she could save everyone, that she could save herself and her mom.

"Would it help if I said I knew your mother?" Shiloh sighed. "She did a wonderful job with the wards here, but they won't last forever."

"You knew my mother?" Lana asked. "How?"

"Lana," Shiloh said.

How did he know her name? Who was this man?

"Please make a decision. Trust me or don't. We don't have time. I can barely hold this portal open in the middle of Elaine's wards. It's quite taxing."

"Fine," Lana said, her stomach doing nervous flips.

"I'm coming with you." Liam tightened his grip on her hand. She wanted to refuse him, to tell him to stay, but her selfish fears wouldn't let the words leave her mouth. Despite her desire to uncover the truth, the portals still scared her. Going to Faerie still scared her.

"Whatever. Just make it quick," Shiloh said from the hallway.

Lana glanced through the window again as they entered the hallway. "What about Marty?"

Rounding the corner, Lana was surprised to see the strangeness of Shiloh, who stood half-in and half-out of the shadowy portal. His lavender hair was long and straight, falling to his waist. He wore pale-colored fabrics draped across his body and sturdy leather leggings. He reminded her of Legolas, just a little bit, but without the pointed ears. He had an air of arrogance and knowledge about him. His eyes were a vibrant gold, like flickering flames, so much like her father's that the sight made her skid to a stop.

"He'll be fine. The Hollows are most certainly after you. We can check on him once we return to Kaelum. If I need to return for him, then I will—for your sake." He waved a hand with a dismissive flourish.

His words tore her from her grief-ridden thoughts. "Alright." Lana nodded with a determination she didn't feel.

"Good." Shiloh opened his arms wide. A burst of gold flashed from his fingertips and the portal widened and stabilized. "Quickly. Quickly." He leaned against the portal's edge, holding it open with his back and arms as gold continued to trace around the portal from his hands.

"I'm not sure about this." Liam glanced back at the living room where they had been only moments ago.

"Neither am I, but I have to do this. You don't have to come with me." The words came out like a whisper. She had to find her mom, even if she did it alone. This was her only chance. Her legs trembled. She couldn't make him come with her. Wouldn't ask him to come. Taking a deep breath to calm herself, she pulled away from Liam and plunged into the portal, trying desperately not to think about what she was doing, what was happening, or where she'd end up.

She felt weightless, breathless. The only thing she was conscious of was the thudding of her heart—solid, strong, and terrified. Light surrounded her, golden and bright, and then water rushed in, greedily snatching her limbs under. She was sinking in slick algae, choking on unnaturally thick water. She fought, but couldn't help but to succumb to the slime.

Still blinded by the golden light, Lana struggled out of the gunk and it receded from her body, falling away to nothingness, leaving her gasping for breath on rough sand.

CHAPTER 10

Lana

On her hands and knees, Lana blinked heavily, fingers digging into warm sand. Taking another deep breath, she searched her surroundings. The familiar trees and lights of her childhood home were all gone, replaced by a completely alien landscape—a sky glowing unnaturally blue and a desert of reddish-gray sand that reeked of death. Dunes lined the distant horizon, only broken by strange monoliths of blood-colored stone. Other than the bones of dead trees, the landscape was silent. Empty. She was alone.

Her heart sped in frantic, terrified beats. Only a few feet away, the sand smoothed out into a flat plane before it dropped away into a hole that plunged deep into the earth. *Had Liam and the strange man fallen into the hole?* Lana crawled forward. She felt wrong and clumsy. Too hot. Empty. Her thoughts wouldn't string together, but simply thrummed with sensations she couldn't place other than fear. Fear was her constant companion.

As she neared the edge of the hole, a strange pressure built in her gut, like fire. Sand trickled over the edges of the pit, cascading down like waterfalls. She couldn't help but look at the bottom. The drop would easily be deadly, even though a glowing pool of deep water resided at the bottom of the hole, with only a thin shore of dirt and stone around it.

The glow of the water mesmerized her. Some unknown light illuminated from deep within the pool, which was almost perfectly clear. As she stared, a human silhouette became clear. Her heart hammered against her chest. She focused entirely on the silhouette and something inside her shifted, like a weight slipped from her and sank into the ground, a slight relief from that tense feeling inside her.

That figure...it couldn't be Liam. It couldn't be. She squinted at the silhouette and noticed how the flow illuminated its hair, which was much too long to be Liam's and a silvery shade of white, unlike Liam's dark curls. She expected to be relieved as she watched the gentle fluttering of the bright-silver hair that haloed the man's head, but she still felt unsettled. She closed her eyes against the image of the man. *It's not Liam*, she told herself, but her heart would not slow. Her chest ached. Her thoughts raced again. *Fear. Empty. Nothing. Alone.*

She scrambled away from the pit. A wet noise slapped against the sand behind her, and Lana whirled around, shifting into a crouch, ready to run.

Golden light flashed and disappeared, leaving Liam kneeling on the sand behind her. His eyes widened and rolled back.

Lana rushed toward him, throwing herself in his direction as his head lolled back and he fell. "Liam! Liam!" she screamed, desperately trying to catch him.

Unconscious, he hit the ground with a soft thud.

She slid one arm beneath his head and cradled him in her lap. His chest rose and fell with breath. With two fingers against his neck, she felt his pulse—steady and normal, as far as she could tell. Lana brushed her fingers across his cheek and tapped gently. "Liam. Wake up, please," she said, barely able to tamp down her panic.

Another flash of golden light blinded Lana momentarily, but when she opened her eyes, Shiloh stood looking down at her with a tendril of smoke escaping his nostrils.

"What's wrong with Liam?" Her voice wavered, cracking with shrillness in her final words.

Shiloh leaned over, inspecting him. "Nothing to worry about. The magic of Kaelum can be a bit overwhelming to non-fae. His body needs time to acclimate, that's all."

"Then what about me? What about you? We're both human!" Lana shook her head, pulling him closer without thinking.

"Human, yes, but..." Shiloh shrugged. "I'm a Havenite. Living in Kaelum so long leaves us all a bit fae-touched. You, on the other hand...I suspect it's because Elaine was from Haven."

"My mother was from here?" Lana once again thought back to the last time she'd seen her mother. "Is she here? This must be where she came to."

"I certainly hope she's in Kaelum. I—we may need her. Or, at least, we may need her amulet. Have you ever seen her amulet—a silver chain with a red jewel in the center? Does that sound familiar?"

Lana nodded. "She wore it every day. What does an amulet have to do with defeating those monsters?" Sweat beaded on Lana's forehead, and she could already feel the sting of the sun on her skin.

"Well, I hope we won't need it." Shiloh regarded her with narrowed eyes, inspecting the lines of her face and the frown curving her lips. "I think you'll be enough. Either you or your mother's amulet will wake the warrior of Haven—the Keeper of Light. If you want to eradicate the Hollows, you'll need her help," Shiloh said before whistling loudly. The sound pierced the quiet air, making Lana jerk with startled surprise.

"I just want to find my mom—but how am I supposed to help you? Didn't you say that we would help each other? Also, why did you whistle? More magic?" Lana wiped at her face and leaned forward, shielding Liam from the sun with her body.

"Waking the warrior is how you'll help me. I've been trying to find a way to wake Anastasia for years now. We both want the same thing, Lana—for Kaelum to return to the way things ought to be." Shiloh searched the horizon as he spoke. "It's far too hot in this hideous desert. Where is Lu?" He fanned himself with a piece of his robe.

Shiloh sighed in relief as an enormous black horse with its tail held high galloped on a hardened path she hadn't noticed before. It pulled a shaded wagon—small with open-air windows and a pale canvas covering that merely sat on top, blocking the sun from the wooden bed inside and leaving most of the wooden hoops exposed. There were no seats, except the coachman's seat at the front, which also had a small shade.

The horse slowed to a stop and neighed impatiently.

"Yes, yes," Shiloh said. "We'll be quick, Lu."

Lana rushed to her feet. Standing clumsily, she held Liam in her arms. He was far heavier than he looked. She squinted against the sun. It was too hot. Much too hot. She took a wobbling step forward.

Shiloh looked back at her, with a furrowed brow.

A wave of fiery heat rolled over Lana and settled deep in her gut like a pool of molten gold, sparkling and swirling, aching to bubble to the surface and rise from her skin like steam. She felt like her insides were pulled in too many directions. The image of the man in the pit kept rising to the top of her mind. She held on to that image of his hair fluttering in the water—that beautifully morbid image—trying to focus on anything but the overwhelming fire in her veins. *In death, would she be alone like him? If she fell too, would her mother be waiting on the other side of this nightmare?* Blackness crowded her vision. Her ears felt full, muted, until she lost the battle with herself and fainted, collapsing back down on the sand.

CHAPTER II

Lana

The wind brushed against Lana's hair, tossing the blonde locks against her face as she began to rouse from unconsciousness. Slowly, the world came back to her—waning heat from a setting sun seared the desert beyond the little carriage she rode in; the tang of copper and rot wafted from the sands that surrounded her. A muttering voice drifted in and out of her comprehension.

"Down once we get to the temple, Lu," said Shiloh, sitting in the coach seat of the carriage. The horse shook its head, huffing in protest. "I can't take any chances with either of them, whether you like my decisions or not."

The horse blew out a breath and the pair continued to trudge through the desert, while Lana wrestled with her thoughts, putting together the scattered pieces of her mind.

The shadows. Liam. A portal. Her memory clicked into place. Worse than that, she remembered that she wasn't in an unfamiliar desert. She knew exactly where she was. She lifted her head, hoping she was mistaken.

Stretching out to the very edge of the horizon was sand...empty sand. All her nightmares rushed back to her. She'd been here before, chased by hulking brutes of bone and flesh, stained black and wrapped in pulsing red vines and exposed muscle. Her eyes automatically scanned the horizon, but the sun still sat in the pale sky.

The creatures only appeared as the daylight waned. She squeezed her eyes shut, focusing on the gentle rocking of the wagon's movement beneath her and the ache of her body, hoping she could calm her frenzied heartbeats.

In her dreams, the sand had never felt this substantial or warm. She had always been alone with the howls of the nightmare creatures.

Never before had she felt so alive. She felt different—more whole yet shattered at the same time.

Her thoughts were interrupted as the waning sunlight glinted across the sand, piercing her eyes painfully. In the distance, a steepled roof peeked over the top of a dune. The sun scattered along the roof, making the white stone of the roof glitter. With each jostling step, the rest of the building rose from the dunes. It was a temple of white stone, with elaborate twisting pillars and enormous stone doors. Lanterns hung from every corner and glowed a gentle, bioluminescent blue, as if someone had caught a glowing jellyfish and placed it in a hanging jar.

The horse came to an abrupt stop in front of the temple. Shiloh turned to face her, his lavender hair fluttering in the desert breeze.

"Good. You're awake," he said as he approached. "Let's get you inside."

She groaned as he helped her crawl out of the wagon. Her limbs still felt like jelly—unsettled and unstable, malleable clay—and her sides were bruised and aching.

He tsked as he settled her against the side of the wagon. "The portal was a bit rough, it seems. Or maybe the ride here? I'd thought Kaelum wouldn't affect you like this. Something's not quite right." Shiloh went to the horse, removing all the equipment and freeing it from the wagon. He went around to the back, groaning as he pulled Liam from the wagon. He carried him with a grimace and tossed him across the horse's back. "Let's all get inside." He patted the horse's shoulder.

"Where are we?" Lana ventured to ask, though her voice warbled. For a long moment, her eyes didn't leave Liam's unconscious form.

"Lovely question to be asking now," he mused with a mirthless laugh. "Can you walk on your own?"

Lana took a step forward and nearly fell to the ground.

Shiloh frowned, shaking his head as he moved to her side and pulled her against him, draping her arm across his shoulder. "You'll feel better in the temple. I'm certain of it…" He trailed off for a moment, silently pulling her up the stone stairs. "We're in Silvis," he said finally. "One of several nations in Kaelum."

"Are we still on Earth?"

Only a few more steps and they would be at the top. The horse trailed after them, silently carrying Liam.

"Yes." Shiloh paused for a moment as Lana slowed. "Though, that's a bit of a complicated question. We're in a Faerie realm—on Earth, but also not. Faerie defies explanation."

"*A* Faerie realm?" she asked between labored breaths. She'd never climbed so many stairs and especially not in this kind of heat. "So there's more than one? Kaelum is just one of them?"

"Precisely. Kaelum holds many faerie courts, like the Court of Dreams, the Wild Court, the Court of the Abyss, the Court of Bones, the Court of Shadows. Even the Court of Ice is somewhere in Kaelum."

Shiloh pulled her forward into the deliciously cool shade of the temple's roof, and she sighed at the sudden relief from the sun. Once they reached the peak of the stairs, they finally stopped walking, and Shiloh pulled away from her.

Even as he let go of her, letting her lean against the wall of the temple near the door, Shiloh continued to explain, as if lecturing a student. "However, there are plenty of courts in separate realms—the Celestial Court and the Summer Court being the two that come to mind. But there are thousands, if not millions, of faerie courts. For every thought, idea, and aspect of existence on Earth, there is a faerie court. It's quite fascinating, but I've never had the time to study such things."

Lana doubled over, bracing her hands on her thighs as she caught her breath. "What?" she said between inhales. She'd never felt this out of shape in her life and wondered whether her body was even compatible with this world. *Would she die if she stayed too long? What about Liam?*

Shiloh pressed back against one of the pillars, steadying his breathing as well. "Let's save any more questions for after we're inside the temple."

"Then fine. Let's just get inside before the sun sets." Lana spared a glance toward the sky and the sun that sank ever closer to the horizon, trying not to think about her nightmares and the beasts that most certainly would appear once night fell completely.

Shiloh nodded. He placed his hand across the door. At his touch, golden ribbons of light sprang up and twisted into the intricate designs that were carved into the white stone doors. The light spread until the entire entrance was covered in molten light, and then the doors slid inward, scraping against the floor in a well-worn groove.

The golden light drained from the doors and raced along the floor ahead of them as they stepped into the temple. Torches of golden flame exploded to life as they entered, illuminating a small entry room of statues. Shiloh led her farther inside. Candles stood beside rows of glass boxes and flickered to life as the golden lines of magic continued to trace stripes along the floors and walls.

"Convenient," Lana said. *Magic.* She knew she ought to be shocked or terrified—something—but instead, it all just seemed right, familiar in some distant way. If Haven was her mother's home, perhaps it called to her in the same way. She shook her head at her fanciful thoughts. Feyville was home, and she would go back there once everyone was safe again and she'd found her mother.

Shiloh nodded and gestured for her to follow him. The horse trotted in ahead of them and disappeared into the temple as they entered. Lana's heart clenched as Liam disappeared with the horse, but what could she do? She was struggling to walk on her own; she couldn't carry Liam too.

"Where's the horse taking Liam?" Lana asked, clutching at the front of her shirt as nausea continued to wash over her in waves.

"Oh? Lu is just taking him into the sanctuary. We'll be there in just a moment. Don't worry about your friend," Shiloh said without looking at her as he continued a few steps forward.

Lana chewed on the dry skin of her bottom lip, reminding herself to relax. Shiloh knew her mother, knew her apparently better than Lana did. She could trust him. Lana tossed a glance back to the giant, open doors. "Can't you close those things? Won't the creatures will come in?"

Shiloh followed her gaze back to the entrance. "Ah. The Hollows cannot step past the entrance to this sacred ground. There are few things Hollows fear, but chief among those is our magic. As long as the golden light runs through this temple, we are safe."

"If they hate your magic so much, why can't you just get rid of them?"

"Get rid of them?" He scoffed. "I may be powerful, but I couldn't rid this world of Hollows. Perhaps I could take out a hundred or more before my soul succumbed, burning to nothingness. Just opening the gate now to pull you safely through nearly pushed me to the burn."

"The burn?"

"Magic has a cost. For Havenites, if we use it too much, it burns through our souls and we die." Suddenly, Shiloh turned toward her with his brows raised. "How do you even know about the Hollows?"

"I've had dreams—nightmares—of this place."

He flexed his fingers and his gaze intensified. "So, you've had dreams about this place?"

Lana nodded jerkily. She looked back at the sand beyond the safety of the temple, sifting through memories of the landscape in her dreams, but there was nothing significant besides the creatures. Her dreams had always been aimless nightmares of sand, grit in her mouth, screeching cries and suffering. There had never been an escape. "Yeah."

He seemed to want more, for her to explain, but Lana didn't know what to say.

Shiloh sighed, his eyes losing the hopeful light they'd had before. He muttered to himself as he turned away, walking into what Lana could only compare to a sanctuary. It was an enormous room with skylights that lit the rows of glass boxes with warm sunlight. Row after row of glass boxes lined the room. At the far end, a sort of altar stood with another glass box sitting on top. "So Elaine came to get rid of the Hollows before bothering to wake her daughter? What nonsense."

"What do you mean, her daughter? I'm already awake" Lana asked. "Do I have a sister?" As she neared the first row of glass boxes, her breath caught in her throat, and she flinched away. Inside was a skeleton draped in a warrior's armament. Hair and cloth had nearly turned to dust, or—as Lana noticed, leaning closer—perhaps ash. A shield blanketed the lower half of the skeleton and a sword laid atop it. Both were designed with delicate craftsmanship, twisting metals and careful engravings. The shield was emblazoned with a sun crossed by a sword—the symbol reminded her of a recent dream, but it eluded her. At the very top of the glass coffin, a few lines of text were created with small shards of stained glass: *Marcus Cresthallow. Go peaceful into the abyss. Fallen, but not forgotten.*

It wasn't a box—it was a coffin. The room was filled with row after row of glass coffins. *Had these people burned from using magic?* She pulled her eyes from the skeleton reclining in its final resting place and scurried after Shiloh.

"Just come with me. I'll show you." Flickers of golden candlelight danced across his hair.

"Have you not seen my mother?" Shiloh didn't slow, so Lana hurried to follow him deeper into the sanctuary. Her gaze swept around the dimly lit room, taking in row after row of fallen warriors.

"Not for a very long time," he said. "I suspected she had returned to Kaelum, but I've not seen her in over two decades."

Two decades. Had he been a child when her mother was here last? Lana held back from asking. It didn't matter anyway. "So how did you know I was in danger, back at the house?"

Shiloh paused, but didn't turn around; Lana nearly ran into his back. "I've been watching you for some time. You and Elaine are my last hope at waking Anastasia. You're important."

Lana shifted uneasily. *He'd been watching her?* She thought of all the times she'd imagined the weight of a stranger's gaze from the depths of shadows. *Had that been him?* She rubbed a hand across her arm, trying to dispel the chills that ran across her flesh. He was helping her, and he needed her help. *There's nothing sinister about it,* she told herself.

To distract herself, she asked another question, one that kept popping up in the back of her mind, haunting her. "Who was that back in the pit in the desert?"

Shiloh turned toward her with a smile that didn't reach his eyes. "Curious about the boy in the wellspring?"

"Yes, I guess." She shrugged. She didn't even know why it kept haunting her...the man with the silver hair, floating in the water. "How long has he been there? Why hasn't someone fished him out? A dead body can't be good for the water."

"Oh, he's not dead," Shiloh said. "And, he's been there for quite some time—a couple decades, at least. Don't waste your thoughts on him." He turned and continued down the aisle, until he made it to the steps leading to the altar at the far end of the room.

"What? I don't understand." She watched his movements carefully.

With a muttered word in a strange language, a short burst of flame shot from his fingertips, lighting another row of candles along the back wall, illuminating the horse, who still held Liam across his back.

Lana relaxed now that Liam was finally in sight again. But why was he not awake yet? *It had been hours—hadn't it?*

"He fell in." He carefully pulled Liam from the horse's back and rested him on the smooth stone floor. "Unattended children tend to do that sort of thing."

Lana ran a hand across her forehead, pressing two fingers gently against her brows to soothe the anxiety that was trying to consume her. *Liam would be fine.* He just needed to get used to Kaelum. *That was all. It would be fine. It's fine. He's fine.* She refocused on the conversation to distract herself again. "But how is he not dead?"

"The wellspring is pure magic, and quite dangerous. I'm sure he's fine enough. He's likely having wonderful dreams of whatever lies between worlds. It's certainly not worth the risk of trying to pull him from the pool. Who knows what the magic has done to him, let alone what it would do to someone else if they were to touch it. Only the Hollows get near the wellspring, and they've never bothered him. The boy is probably part monster at this point."

"Oh," was all Lana said. She didn't know how else to react. It seemed heartless to leave him out there, but she didn't really understand this world, so what did she know? "When will Liam wake up?" The words tumbled from her lips suddenly.

"Your mother was always much better with this kind of thing—souls, I mean," he gestured to Liam, "than I ever was, so I can only take a guess at how long it will take his soul to acclimate to a Faerie realm. It could be just a few more hours—it could be days. We'll just have to wait and see...and hope we find Elaine quickly." He leaned down and pulled a small hand mirror from a bag on the ground. "Now, let's check on Martin," he said, whispering across the glass.

Lana hurried to his side, climbing the stairs on either side of the altar with careful steps. She couldn't believe she'd forgotten about Marty; even with everything going on around her, she should have remembered. He was the one really in danger. She stopped, hovering by Shiloh's side as the mirror rippled like water and the house came into view.

It was still night and the lights shone brightly across the yard. Marty stood in the middle of the front yard with his sword in his hand, tip against the grass. He was alone. The darkness past the fence was completely empty. He was safe. Lana sighed, and Shiloh shook the mirror, dispelling the image before he returned it to the bag on the floor.

"As I said—the Hollows were after you. Now, on to the important matters." He placed his hands on the lid to another glass coffin, but this one was different than the rest. The sides were decorated with elaborate stained glass. Roses and suns danced on the artful sepulture.

Lana forced herself to look down. Candlelight illuminated the face of a young woman. She truly seemed to be only in a deep sleep. Her chest rose and fell in almost imperceptible movements with breath. Lana traced her fingers along the epitaph at the top of the glass tomb.

Anastasia, The Keeper of Light

Lana couldn't look away, couldn't move. The face she stared down at looked oddly like her own. She would have easily been persuaded to think this girl was her twin. Unlike Lana, Anastasia had the body of a warrior, even in this sleep. Her hair was long, but braided into twists and loops that were pinned neatly to her head like a crown.

She wore sturdy pants and a light tunic, but unlike the other warriors, Anastasia didn't have a shield. Only a sword lay in her coffin, with the blade pointed down toward her feet. Her strong hands, rough with scars and callouses, wrapped lightly around the hilt at her navel.

Shiloh knelt beside the coffin. "Magic comes at a price. The greater the magic, the greater the price. Commander Creon had hoped to keep the Hollows trapped here in the desert and then to escape back to our ancestral homeland—your world." Shiloh placed his hands lovingly across the top of the coffin.

"So she was the price." Lana frowned. Their voices echoed, bouncing off the stone walls of the sanctuary, lending some strange finality to their words.

"And now, I need you to wake her," Shiloh said.

"How am I supposed to do that? And what about the spell on her? You just said it keeps the creatures trapped here? The Hollows?" Lana glanced over her shoulder, looking into the shadows still lingering in the corners—the candlelight only a soft glow over the room.

Shiloh scoffed. "The wall did nothing to help the Silvids, not that Creon ever knew, safe in another world. The Hollows kept appearing all across Silvis. The only change was now our people weren't around to cull the numbers of the beasts."

"But, I can't do this. I can't wake her. I don't have magic. We need to find my mother's amulet." Lana shook her head. *Why did he think she could do it?* She was nobody, nothing.

"You can." Shiloh's voice was rough with intense emotion. "I've spent decades looking for a way to break her curse. Then, I found you." Shiloh delicately pushed the glass lid from Anastasia's coffin until it rested at an angle on the ground nearby.

"What's so special about me?" Lana muttered.

Shiloh paused, staring into the coffin for a long moment before he said, "Anastasia is Elaine's daughter."

"So, she's my sister?" Lana looked down at the warrior. She couldn't deny their resemblance.

"Your connection is what will break this spell. I'm certain of it."

"And if it does, then she'll destroy the Hollows? But what if I can't? Will you still help me find my mother?" No matter what, she wanted to find her. Once Liam woke, they could search together. It would be even better if the warrior woke and ran off to defeat the Hollows; then Lana could focus on finding her mother, if she was even alive.

"Just try," he pleaded. "Can't you feel it? The warmth pulsing in your veins? Close your eyes, feel it. Please."

She looked at the woman again. Her face was frozen in a tense expression—furrowed brows and a slight frown. What would it feel like to be trapped like this for years? Did she dream? Or was she stuck in a perpetual nightmare? The thought left her feeling clammy. Lana couldn't leave Anastasia trapped in some hell-scape in her mind. She had to try.

Lana closed her eyes, and Shiloh released her arm, kneeling back down at Anastasia's side. Lana was a bit surprised to realize she could feel something. In the pit of her stomach, a completely foreign fluttering feeling churned in waves, with each wave another bout of nausea assailed her. As Lana focused on that fluttering, it became less fragile, until it was a warm energy that unfurled throughout her entire body, washing away the nausea with a gentle golden fire that rushed through her veins. She remembered when she'd first woken on the sand—that fire, that molten gold. Stepping into this realm had woken something in her. Suddenly Lana felt certain of one fact, she *could* wake Anastasia, and she must.

When she opened her eyes, she saw Anastasia's face again, but now she noticed that the gentle glow on her face wasn't from the altar candles as she had thought, but from within. Anastasia was glowing with golden light from within.

She wondered whether Anastasia would disappear if she touched her, if she brushed her fingers across the soft, exposed cheek of the young woman, who was like a distorted reflection of herself. Would she wake with just a touch? Lana felt compelled. The fiery magic that played beneath her skin consumed her as she stretched her fingertips toward the glow emanating from Anastasia.

Daylight erupted around the pair. Lana felt the warm skin of Anastasia's face against her hands, her careful braids twisting in her fingertips. The sensation was much like what she'd felt when she first came to Kaelum—a sinking, a surrounding. Everything was warmth and light. Lana felt weightless. She was nothing. There was nothing.

The ground shook as she returned to consciousness. Lana's eyes opened, fluttering and struggling against the weight of her eyelids. The blue light that had once filtered in from the skylights dimmed and faded, leaving the sanctuary bathed in the golden light of the candles, with only darkness beyond the windows.

Shiloh glanced up. "The spell wall has broken. It worked." He smiled and stared down at her. Relief, love, and panic battled for dominance on his face.

She furrowed her brows and pushed herself up. Lana had ended up on the ground. Or, at least, she thought she had been on the ground, but her hands met smooth glass.

Her body ached, each muscle groaned with forced motion. Lana looked down at herself and realized she was no longer herself. A sword sat heavily in her lap and she stared out through unfamiliar eyes.

CHAPTER 12

Vas

Vas woke, suspended in the depths of liquid magic—the wellspring. The sound of soft currents drifted past his ears and he realized he couldn't feel his body. He was weightless. Nothing. He was consciousness floating in a sea of luminescent blue.

Memories swirled in his head, flashes of images mixed together—Athan sending him to the desert, the guards falling to the jaws of the Hollows before they even made it to Haven. The horde had swarmed them at the first hint of twilight. They'd been so close to the temple—the main entrance to Haven.

His mother had wanted him to stay out of the war, but he hadn't listened. *His mother.* Vas's heart clenched. His parents must be worried. Athan would be disappointed in him; he'd been basically useless against that many Hollows.

Shadowy beasts had chased him, like dogs herding an errant sheep—snarling, fanged creatures. *Nowhere to go. Empty desert.* He clutched his head as the memories culminated in one terrifying moment—he jumped into the wellspring to escape the snapping jaws of the Hollows. Since that moment, the depths of the magical pool had been his prison, trapped in a dream of another world, until now.

He opened his mouth, and the liquid rushed in, filling his lungs with the sparks of its magic. It tasted bittersweet, like an iced coffee or buttery pastry filled with dark chocolate. His limbs were heavy. He couldn't control them. Far above, he heard a voice...a familiar voice. In fact, he was certain now that she was the reason he had woken. The memories overtook him again—memories of that other world in his dream. He didn't recognize the landscape. Thick trees broken by empty fields and marshes, but she was there in that other world. That voice was there.

Buzzing with the lightning of the wellspring, Vas finally regained control of his body. He clawed at the water, dragging himself to the surface of the glowing pool. Each movement was agony, aching stiffness. His lungs remembered their desire for air—fresh, thin oxygen.

He broke the surface in a rush of bubbles, as if the wellspring had begun to boil around him. A part of him wanted to stay in the comforting embrace of the sludge and the dreams he'd had there, but the wellspring wouldn't let him. The water grew more solid around him, pushing him toward the shore. It propelled him up in a sudden wave and spit him onto the stone, where he lay, gasping for air.

Vas rolled on to his back and looked up at the sky. Dusk was beginning to settle, but there was a gentle, blue light to the sky that seemed unnatural, like magic. The sky had never looked like this before. *What happened while he slept?*

Stars emerged into existence, dappling the sky beyond that strange blue light. Night was dangerous in the desert. Falling into the wellspring had saved him from the Hollows before, but now there might not be an escape. When the light of the sun finally disappeared below the horizon, he would be alone with the sand and the things that lived among the dunes—the Hollows.

He could easily escape the deep pit of the wellspring if he shifted into a bird, so he pushed himself up to his feet, moving as quickly as his stiff limbs would take him, and tried to shift. His body twisted and bubbled unnaturally. His arms stretched into wings far too heavy for flight and then shrank into leathery bat wings. The magic wouldn't obey him. After several failed attempts, where his magic ran away from him, exploding into shapes he hadn't quite intended, Vas gave up and made his way to the stairs, trying to push down the panic that something was wrong with his magic. Magic had always come easily, especially shifting. *How would he get home safely without it?*

The stone stairs led all the way to the mouth of the pit, which he assumed had been cut into the walls by the academy archaeologists who uncovered the wellspring. He pressed onward, heading up the stairs. The stone felt steady at first, but the farther up he climbed, the less secure the stone became. Rocks broke free and tumbled down, clattering on the ground far below. His throat stung and sweat poured from his skin, but he'd barely gotten even halfway up the enormous crater.

The stairs went on and on. If he didn't remember falling into the wellspring, he wouldn't have believed he'd survived the fall. For a moment, he questioned his existence. He patted his hands together and tapped them on his chest, feeling the solidness of his own body and the strong beat of his heart. He was alive, for now.

Even after he finally reached the top, he'd still need to find a way home. His memories were still messy, and trying to sort through them made his head throb with the effort. When the archaeologists had first uncovered the wellspring, he had been a child. He thought back on the map of Silvis. Silvis was an island that surrounded a desert island in a C shape. The wellspring was in the center of the desert, so the archaeologists must have taken a boat, meaning perhaps there was still a way back to the mainland at the coast. *But from which side?*

The capital was to the west of the desert, so that made the most sense, but no one in the capital had a reason to come to the desert, especially now. *Would the archaeologists have built a dock or left boats close to the academy?* Vas couldn't remember where the academy was built. He'd always had private tutors, so the academy hadn't mattered to him. He furrowed his brows in thought, wishing he had studied the geography of Silvis closer in his youth.

Vas continued to sort through his memories. After the wellspring was uncovered, the Hollows began to appear. Back then, the Hollows were almost unheard of—just a legend in old Silvid tales. He'd found out the hard way they weren't a legend. The memory of the horde chasing him, howling, sands shifting unnaturally beneath his feet, caused him to miss a stair and he nearly tripped.

Night was falling hard. A significant number of stars already sparkled in the vast sky that stretched endlessly above him. Vas was almost at the top when he heard the first screech. The sound was vaguely human, as if speech could be dragged from the horrid jaws of the Hollows. He pushed himself harder, running up the last few stairs. The Silvid temple that marked the entrance to Haven was out in the western desert. It shouldn't be far from here. If he could just get into the temple, he could hide at least until sunrise or see if the Havenites would help him. Would they help him? His clothes were ruined and he had no identification. Without knowing he was the prince, would they be willing to help a Brynian stranger? At this moment, he wished he hadn't been such a recluse.

When Vas finally reached the top of the pit and stepped out onto the open sand, he could see Hollows on the horizon, like wavering dots rolling up and down distant dunes. Their howls filled the air, twisting like storm clouds. The Hollows hadn't seen him yet, but there was no avoiding it. He needed a place to hide, but he was completely in the open.

He racked his brain and crouched low to the ground, gasping for breath after his long climb up the stairs. He didn't have the energy to fight the Hollows, or run from them, and his magic was too unstable to use. He'd have to outsmart them, though he didn't think outsmarting the beasts would be that difficult in theory. From what he knew, they were crazed, rabid things, like wild animals. The Hollows craved flesh and had keen senses, but like most animals, he hoped instinct was all they had.

They would be on top of him in a matter of minutes. Already, the putrid scent of rotting meat was growing stronger, brought to him on the wind. With the desert wind blowing in his face, Vas had an idea. The Hollows would eventually catch his scent; it was futile to think otherwise. But confusing them might work, at least long enough to get to the temple.

Hoping it would buy him at least a little time, Vas removed the shredded rags from his torso that had once been a shirt. Easily, he pulled the rags in half. One piece, he held to the ground under a rock at his feet. The rag fluttered up with the wind, waving like a flag.

The other half he held to the wind and let go. The rag tumbled across the desert with the wind, heading south. He knew it would go far with the wind as strong as it was. With any luck, he hoped the tattered fabric would keep tumbling across the sand for the next few hours. Then Vas started to make his way west, keeping low to the ground. He moved as quickly as his sore legs could carry him. He didn't dare climb to the top of any dune, worried the Hollows would spot him.

The frenzied yowl of the Hollows let him know exactly when they had found his rags. Their occasional screeches and bestial murmurings carried across the sand and twisted into a chorus of howls. He kept pushing, desperately trying to put distance between himself and the Hollows.

Their howls became violent, screeches of a battle beginning, but one sound cut across all of them. A single, commanding bark ripped through the noise of the frenzied creatures and they all fell silent. He didn't have time to wonder what had happened, so he just kept going, hoping he'd get to safety before the Hollows appeared.

Vas moved in and out of the dunes, climbing halfway up one side of a dune, crawling and clinging to the other side of the dune, just to slide down on his bare stomach. The silence remained heavy on the desert, and he pushed himself harder, not knowing when the Hollows might appear—how close they might be already. The sand bit at his flesh and covered him. His hands and feet were raw from clawing at the sand. Each breath was agonizing and filled with grit.

He kept moving in the eerie silence for hours. His body was nearly at its limit. The night was here in full now, and Vas had no idea how far he'd come, or how much longer he'd have to go before he reached the temple. He decided to take a risk and started to climb to the top of the nearest dune.

With one final heave, Vas stood atop a dune and looked across the desert. He had visited the desert on several occasions before the Hollows appeared, but he had never seen it like this. The sun had set completely, leaving behind only the rose hues of dusk against the horizon. A small sliver of moon hung in the sky, illuminating and casting shadows in the endless dark of rolling dunes. The sands were empty, or at least more empty than he remembered from his escape that night, making him wonder how much time had passed since he'd plummeted to the bottom of the wellspring.

The night was still, and the Hollows were nowhere in sight. Plants had withered away to nothing. All that remained were the rolling, ever-shifting dunes of stained sand and the smell of copper and rust. The desert wasn't how he remembered it at all. Now, this was a place of blood and bone.

From his perch, he saw the temple and sighed in relief. Somehow, he had made it, and the doors were open. Vas stepped forward and slid down the side of the dune, heading toward the ancient Silvid temple. The building loomed above him like a giant. His jaw relaxed as he took a slow inhale. The foundation was solid rock. He followed the steps up to the doors, running his hand across the twisted designs on the pillars that framed the entrance.

The designs were so intricate and perfectly sculpted that Vas thought it obvious Silvid magic had been used in its construction, which surprised him. Silvid legends were full of tales depicting the evils of magic—like the story of King Dae. To the Silvids, magic was dangerous. Magic was sin. Vas never understood that line of thinking. He used magic all the time and nothing bad had ever happened to him...excepting his current predicament.

For a moment, Vas considered whether the temple could have been made some other way, but that moment's thought passed quickly. If it had been built by magic, and he was certain it had been, only Silvids could use manipulation magic like this, working with stone and earth. His thoughts wandered and he wondered what Silvis had been like before the wellspring was sealed back in the Dae Era.

Vas shook off his thoughts. He knew he should be on his guard. The doors were open, and he had no way of knowing whether Hollows lurked in the depths of what he had hoped to be his safe haven until morning. The sanctuary was dark, but the smell of recently burning candles was fresh in the air. Someone was here. Hopefully, they were still alive and hadn't become dinner for the Hollow horde.

His foot crossed the threshold of the open doors, and the world shook, quaking beneath him. He dropped to the ground and covered his head in a moment of panic. *What was happening?* Suddenly, that strange, gentle light of the sky shattered, and the night became dark and ominous. At the far-off horizon, he could just barely hear the howling excitement of the Hollows in the wake of this new, deep night.

CHAPTER 13

Lana

Shiloh pressed his fingers against her cheek. "Anastasia?"

Lana sat in the open coffin with her legs stretched out in front of her. The cold glass pressed against the bare skin of her arms. She pulled her hands into her lap, making herself smaller—or as small as possible for a warrior in a glass coffin.

She couldn't speak, didn't dare speak.

Shiloh looked deep into her eyes and his hand dropped from her cheek. The hopeful look in his eyes drained away, leaving his expression empty. His mouth was a slack line, and his shallow breath barely raised his chest. Shiloh heaved himself up to his feet, refusing to look at her.

"I'm sorry," Lana managed to squeak. Her voice was rougher and a few notes deeper than she was used to hearing. "What happened?"

Shiloh flinched, tensing up until his shoulders were almost by his ears. He faced the wall with his eyes shut tight.

Lana tried to stand, but stumbled, tumbling out of the coffin and onto the icy stone. On her hands and knees, Lana crawled toward the steps that led down to the altar, twisting to sit at the top of the stairs. "I don't know what I did. I tried to use magic like you asked and..."

Shiloh sighed and turned back to face her. "You did nothing but give yourself to the spell already in place...which you broke, by the way. I thought you were the key. I thought Elaine had..." He shook his head. "I suppose not. Anastasia must still be in the amulet." He clenched his fists and shoved them in his pockets.

"What are you talking about? I broke a spell? Why am I not in my own body?" Lana rubbed her hands up and down her arms, willing warmth into her aching muscles. She wished she had a blanket. Despite the fires that were lit around the room, the cold of the desert seeped into her skin.

Shiloh waved his hand dismissively. "The spell wall keeping the Hollows in the desert is gone, which also means I won't be able to open a portal between worlds as easily."

"I'm stuck here?" Lana asked. She hadn't been planning to go home—she still needed to find her mom and wake Anastasia to defeat the monsters, but losing the possibility of leaving made her chest feel tight.

"For now? Yes, but if it's any consolation that means the Hollows are stuck too." Shiloh crossed his arms and his speech took on a lecturing tone. "For a mage to purposefully create a gate between realms, they need a powerful in-between. Without a powerful one, there's no telling where a gate might lead. The in-between of life and death is the most powerful. Any mage, even the Hollows apparently, could access it, but now your little town is safe. Isn't that what you wanted?"

It had been. She wanted Marty safe and her home safe, but now she and Liam couldn't go home? "Then what do I do now?" Lana asked herself aloud.

Shiloh answered her quiet question. "You help me. We find Elaine. She'll know how to wake Anastasia and, I'm sure, how to get you back home."

Her mom. Lana nodded, knowing he was right. Her mom would fix everything. Lana just needed to find her, and to do that she would need to trust the strange man in front of her.

Shiloh stared up at the ceiling and tapped his foot slowly on the stone as he muttered to himself incoherently. Suddenly, his focus dropped to Lana. "How do you feel?"

"Fine?" She knotted her fingers together and tucked them into her lap.

"Tired? Drained? Mentally foggy? How do you feel?" he asked again. Standing several feet away from her, he lingered, unmoving, by Anastasia's empty tomb.

"Well, I'm fine. I guess I feel a bit wobbly and awkward, but I'm not tired. Actually, I feel the opposite of tired. I feel kind of..." Lana paused, searching for the right word. "Powerful."

Shiloh nodded curtly. "Of course. Anastasia is much stronger than you, so it's only natural to feel overwhelmed and clumsy. She spent decades training as a warrior. You wouldn't, couldn't, have any grace in such a different form." He paced back and forth behind her as his murmured thoughts spiraled out of Lana's hearing.

She watched him pace. She knew she should feel something—fear, shock, anxiety...something, anything—but this was like a vivid dream. Even though this world felt more real than it ever had before. In Feyville, Lana had gone about the world in a shade of gray. Colors were less vibrant back home. Smells were gentler. Sensations were less intense.

But in Kaelum? She had never felt an ache as exquisite as her sore muscles in this moment, or the floor as solid and smooth as the stone. In this moment, Kaelum felt like a homecoming—a place she'd always known and had always meant to be. Surreal. So, instead of analyzing those thoughts, Lana did what she did best—shoved it deep down in her mind. That was a later problem. At the moment, she had a more pressing problem.

She was stuck in someone else's body, who could save the realms from being overrun by the monsters from her nightmares—not to mention, her mother was somewhere in this faerie realm. Find her mother, wake the warrior, save the world. Things were much simpler yesterday. Lana sighed, rubbing her fingers across her eyebrows in attempt to dissipate the stress accumulating there.

Shiloh stopped pacing and stared at the floor. "We only have one feasible course of action," he said. "First, we need to find Elaine's amulet. Then, depending on the outcome of that, I suppose we will need—" He paused. "We'll come to that when we come to it."

Lana looked down at her hands—scarred and calloused. *How had this happened? How had she ended up in this body?* She had so many questions. Her eyes shifted around the room, expecting to find Liam still sleeping against the wall, but he wasn't there. Her body wasn't anywhere in the room either. She could feel the panic rising, making her heart race with worry and the slightest hope—hope that Liam had gotten used to being in a Faerie realm and woken.

"Where's Liam? Where's my body?" She took a deep breath to calm herself.

Shiloh glanced up, jerked from whatever thoughts he'd been thinking. "Ah?" He blinked, refocusing on her. "My associate took..." He waved a hand in the air, searching for the right words. "You...your body and the boy down to my apartment in Haven while you were still unconscious. I didn't expect that you'd wake in Anastasia's body. Even the best laid plans..." He sighed. "You and your friend are safe, so there is no need to worry. Instead, let's focus on next steps."

"Did Liam wake?" Lana shifted uncomfortably on the stone steps.

"He was still unconscious when my associate left, so it's unlikely."

Silence fell between them for a painfully long moment.

She didn't want to think about the possibility that something was wrong. *Liam would be fine. He had to be fine.* They were both stuck here, so all she could do was take the next step forward. Finally, Lana spoke. "You said we need to find the amulet?"

Shiloh tapped a finger on the side of the glass coffin. "The amulet is either with Elaine or somewhere in Haven—likely one of her workshops. Checking her workshops in Haven will be a significantly easier task, so we'll start there, though I've checked them many times in the last few decades...maybe something has changed." A far-off expression returned to his eyes.

"But what do I do?" Lana asked.

"A piece of Anastasia's soul should still be somewhere in that body. Try talking to her? All of the magic I've used getting you here has been taxing. I require rest. We'll leave for Haven at first light." He walked to the other side of the altar, just about ten feet away.

Talk to a piece of her sister's soul? How could she do that? Nothing Shiloh said made sense. Her mind turned to Liam again. *He's fine,* she reassured herself. "Haven?" Lana asked, letting this new information distract her from her thoughts.

"Our home." He sighed. "Where all the humans in Silvis lived. But it's in ruins now—a mere shell of its glorious past."

"You don't look very human," Lana said.

Shiloh scoffed, dragging a hand through his long hair. "Yes, well, magic does change us a bit. The more we use it, the more it changes." His fingers fluttered over the tip of his ear, smoothing over the perfectly round shell.

"But Anastasia doesn't look so—" Lana struggled for words as she stared at Shiloh again, noting his delicate features and the shimmering, lavender tint of his hair.

Shiloh twisted a lock of hair through his fingers. "Ah. Well, perhaps I used magic a bit more than the average Havenite did, or likely ever would. I've tried so many spells, trying to wake Anastasia." He dropped his hand from his hair.

"If Haven is for humans, what's the rest of this place? Just Hollows?"

"I suppose so. The desert has long been abandoned by the fae—even before the Havenites abandoned it." Shiloh sighed. "You should try to talk to Anastasia. She could explain this world better than I ever could, I'm sure. She always said my explanations were lacking...interest." He smiled wistfully as he turned away, reaching next to Anastasia's coffin, where there was a pile of blankets.

For a brief moment, she tried. Lana closed her eyes and looked deep within herself, trying to dredge up something that felt foreign, to find a piece of Anastasia. But she felt only the yawning darkness that shielded herself from the emotions she didn't want to acknowledge. Lana gave up with a slow exhale.

Glancing at Shiloh, where he still stood staring into Anastasia's empty coffin, Lana whispered, "I'm sorry I'm not her."

"I'm sorry too," he said softly. His voice wavered.

"How did you know I wasn't her?"

"Your expressions, your confusion, are unnatural on her face. She is something that can't be replicated. Anastasia was fierce and full of life. The closest woman I've ever met to her ferocity was General Bludeg, and of course they were...close, so that was expected, I guess." He took a shaking breath. "Also, your eyes are wrong. I don't understand the magic of it, but your eyes are not the same as hers. Like the rest of our people, Anastasia's eyes are gold, while yours are dark brown."

"You said I'm one of your people, but why aren't my eyes gold?"

"My guess—you've lived in a world without magic so long that your soul has forgotten it."

"Who even were 'our people'? What do you even mean?"

Shiloh's inhale was audible. "You ask entirely too many questions that would take hours to explain in a thorough or meaningful way—magical theory, history, founding myths. I don't even understand why your eyes are the wrong color. I only have guesses. Will that suffice?"

"You're the one who dragged me into this." Lana crossed her arms, as a frown pulled at her lips. She didn't want to be a bother, but there was so much she didn't know. Maybe she was pushing him too much, asking too much of him.

"Nevertheless, there will be plenty of time for discussion on the way to Haven. I'm going to rest, quietly. Try to do the same." Shiloh rubbed a hand over the back of his neck as he moved to the piles of blankets nearby.

"Okay."

Shiloh picked up several folded lengths of fabric. After a moment of hesitation, he tossed one bit of fabric—a fleecy blanket—toward Lana before he retreated to a spot along the wall and made a bed of blankets in the corner.

Lana frowned and picked up the blanket and held it to her chest. She tilted her head back, eyes drifting across the vaulted ceiling to the skylights. Night had fallen completely. Lana wondered whether the moon was full, or whether this place even had a moon, or whether there were many moons. *What was Kaelum really like? Was she safe here? Was Liam safe down in Haven?*

The silence of the sanctuary left Lana alone with the thoughts she tried desperately to ignore. She wasn't home anymore, and she had no idea where she was. Kaelum was just a name, and this desert was from her nightmares. She would be lost on her own.

Kaelum felt real. She kept coming back to that thought—that this was reality. A heart thumped in her chest and air moved freely in and out of her lungs as she breathed the foreign air. She could smell the candles, most of which had lost their flames and now only emitted a thin wisp of smoke. Though the body wasn't her own, she felt incredibly alive in it. She flexed her fingers and stared at the calloused palms.

She wanted to see the night sky. If she didn't leave the temple, she was safe. Shiloh had assured her of that, so Lana pushed up from the stairs, trying to make her movements silent. She crept away from the altar and back to the entrance of the sanctuary.

In Anastasia's body, she felt different—stronger, more confident in her movements. Her arms were bound by muscle, enough to carry the sword that had been at her side. Lana, however, left the sword by the coffin. She figured there was no point in carrying a sword she didn't know how to use. Though she fought with an odd longing to have the weapon at her waist, she reminded herself that she was safe here. She smiled as she slipped into the shadows of the temple's front room. To feel safe in the shadows was new and exhilarating. She hadn't felt like this since her mother left.

Only one of the torches remained lit, flickering in the corner near the doors. Her blood seemed to spark with lightning, and she enjoyed this new experience. It was a true escape from the small town she'd lived in. *Home.* She frowned. That place hadn't been home since her mother left, but without Liam, Kaelum could never be better.

The front room of the temple was exactly as it had been earlier, but a bit darker without the other torches lit. Daylight that had once poured in was completely gone. Beyond the open doorway, night cloaked the desert in frigid shadows. Stars filled the sky. Lana had never seen so many stars, bright clusters against the void. She moved closer to the entrance, peering out across the dunes.

She silently admired the night for a moment before she felt the weight of eyes on her and whirled around. She peered into the entry room. The sparse torchlight flickered across the statues in the room, but didn't touch the dark corners. Her gaze delved into the shadows, but she saw no one.

Lana ran her hands down her sides, searching for something hidden in her warrior's garb that could be used as a weapon. There was nothing. Hoping her imagination was running wild again, Lana backed toward the sanctuary. She moved in circles as she went, trying to never keep her back turned to any corner for long. She took slow steps, but halfway to the sanctuary, fear seized her, and she sprinted the rest of the way.

Lana burst into the sanctuary, and the flickering candle-light enveloped her with its safety and warmth. She tossed a glance toward Shiloh, but he was still curled up on the floor, motionless in his pile of blankets. Pressing a hand against her chest to slow her breathing, she reminded herself that there was no reason to worry. Shiloh had said that the Hollows couldn't enter the temple, so she was safe here. It was just her imagination.

She had been so certain that something had been in the room with her, though. She returned to the glass coffin and picked up the sword, buckling the sheath around her hips and fitting the blade at her side. The weight of it was comforting and familiar.

Armed, Lana felt more confident, so she returned to the doorway that led into the shadowy entryway. Standing on the edge of the light, she looked over her shoulder toward Shiloh again, but he hadn't moved. She grabbed a lit candle from the top of one of the pedestals that led down the aisle. With a deep breath, she plunged back into the darkness of the entry room.

Drawing the sword and holding it awkwardly, she scanned the dark corners of the room and the shadows cast by the statues, searching for the source of her unease. She held the candle high, casting a dim light on the statues and cold stone. Unconsciously, she held her breath as she turned the light around the room, as if she could sneak up on whatever stalked her from the shadows. Debris littered the floor—some shelves still stood, while others were broken and splintered across the stone.

She moved deeper into the room, exploring the turns and nooks that were hidden by the shelves and statues. The distinct thud of flesh against stone echoed behind her, and she spun around. Wax from her candle splashed across her hand and onto the floor. Lana inhaled sharply, biting back a pained yelp. The light flickered and nearly sputtered out.

When the flame steadied, Lana was still alone in her corner of the room. She held the sword out in front of her.

"Hello?" she whispered.

She stood in the silence, with only the flickering candlelight as her companion, and almost laughed at herself. Even in the safety of the temple, she imagined she saw the shadow creatures, hiding just out of sight.

She knew she should give up on her exploration of the front room and her imaginary monsters in the shadows, but she hesitated. In the shadowy room with the desert just beyond, her fears plagued her. Something was in the room with her.

CHAPTER 14

Vas

V as sat in the darkest corner of the statue room. His body felt wrong—skin too tight, muscles in places he didn't remember. Even trying to process his thoughts and sensations made his head ache with the effort. Voices echoed from the other room, but he couldn't gather the courage to seek their help. He was tired, half-naked and dirty, not to mention a Brynian. No one but his parents and Athan had truly ever offered him help. Then, there was Anastasia, for that brief moment, on the dance floor.

He could have sworn the voice in the other room sounded like her, but something was off, so it couldn't be. In the dim light of the golden candles, it was impossible to really tell, so instead of approaching the pair, he hid. His mind wandered, stuck on the faint remnants of his dreams in the wellspring. *He'd needed to protect someone there. He'd—* The memories shattered as a sudden wave of pain rushed over him.

He gripped his head as if he could force that pain away. His temples throbbed and images surfaced again. Images from that other place. Vas slipped into a crouch and leaned against the stone wall, trying to keep his head straight, but the flashes of color kept playing in his mind. The frustration of incomplete images and wisps of thoughts tightened his face, and he forgot to breathe, leaving his lungs searing.

Vas gave in. He stopped fighting against the pain, the images, the memories of the other place. The loneliness. His heart ached. Even in his wellspring dreams, he was lonely, except for the one bright spot—her. He saw her face clearly, then. Anastasia? But not quite. As he tried to hold on to the image of her face, the pain overwhelmed him until his thoughts slipped away and he was left quivering in the dark corner of the temple.

He took a deep breath, and sank further onto the floor, letting the cold stone overtake his sensations. He focused on that cold and on the pain that still lingered in his head. Vas only had a moment of reprieve before he heard footsteps approaching. He crawled to the closest corner, pushing himself as deep into the dark as he could, and watched.

Even with the candle, the dimness obscured most of her features. She didn't seem to be a Silvid. Probably one of the Havenites. *Should he approach?* But he might scare her. No one wanted to find a stranger in an unexpected place—especially not in the dark—but here they were, in the dark.

She was nearly at the door. If he didn't do something now, she'd slip back into the sanctuary. The light from the larger room put her in shadow. But her silhouette, her voice... *It couldn't be, could it?*

Despite his anxious run-through of plans and horrendous outcomes, he couldn't help but speak. "Anastasia?" he said, almost in a whisper.

The woman inhaled so sharply that specks of saliva caught in her windpipe and she choked. She scrambled away from the voice as she regained her composure and pointed the wavering tip of the sword out toward the darkness.

"Wait," he said again. "I didn't mean to scare you." His voice was soft.

She glanced back toward the sanctuary, where her companion still curled on the floor. "Who are you? Why are you here?" Her words came out in a rush.

Vas stood. He felt drawn to her, like a rope tied to his bones tugged him forward. He moved closer, but stuck to the shadows, afraid to show his face—his horns, marking him as different. People feared different. She held the candle out in front of her and the fragile, excited hope he'd held evaporated, leaving only confusion in its place.

"Are you...? You look exactly like Anastasia—but your eyes." Something else about her seemed different. *Was it her expression?* He'd never seen fear on Anastasia's face, but in truth he'd only met her the once. *How long had he been dreaming in the wellspring?* That question haunted him.

She shifted nervously. "I'm not Anastasia. I'm her sister—Lana. Who are you? What are you doing here?"

"I'm just trying to get home." He paused before he added, "You can call me Vas." Would she know him—Prince Vasileios of Silvis? Would she be more wary of a prince who knew her sister or a strange Brynian fae? He didn't want to scare her off when, now that she'd already discovered him, she might be able to help him. What was he supposed to do?

Lana adjusted her grip on the sword, keeping it pointed at him. "And so you're creeping around in the dark?"

"Well, yes. Better to creep around in the dark than to be eaten by Hollows." Despite the dark, horrible situation he was in, Vas was still smiling while he hid in the shadowy corners, far from the light of Lana's candle. Something about her was endearing, familiar in every way, but he pushed those thoughts firmly from his mind as an impossibility he wouldn't entertain.

"Those things can't come inside the temple." She lifted the candle higher as she stepped forward.

Instinctually, Vas shifted backward, away from the light. *What if she didn't want to talk to him once she saw his horns—saw that he wasn't a Silvid?*

"The Hollows can't come in here?" He was skeptical, but relieved.

Lana's gaze shifted to the open doorway. Vas watched as her eyes roved over the endless sands. "The horrible screeching monsters? Shiloh said they can't enter 'sacred ground.'"

Sacred ground? Ridiculous. The only thing Hollows feared was fire and light, which included the Havenites' flaming magic. *Did the people of Haven consider their magic some kind of divine blessing or was her companion full of grandiose ideas?* Vas rolled his eyes. Humans were so strange. "That makes perfect sense."

"Does it?" Lana's sword drooped, brushing against the stone with a metallic click.

"Sure," Vas replied.

Silence stretched between them. The wind from the desert drifted through the window, chilling the air. *It should be much colder,* Vas thought. *Another benefit of the temple?* He wondered what kind of magic ran in the walls.

"Come out into the light," Lana said, turning away from the doorway.

"What if I don't want to?" He felt quite comfortable in his dark corner, after all.

"Why wouldn't you want to? Are you one of the creatures or something?" She steadied her sword again, waving it in his direction.

"I'm not a Hollow."

Lana raised the candle above her head, trying to force the light to reach farther. "Are you going to kill me?"

Without thinking, Vas responded. "Never."

"Then come out."

He sighed deeply and pushed himself up and into the light. He prepared for the worst, but he still didn't expect her reaction.

"Oh," she said simply, letting her hand dip back down so that the candle rested near her waist.

"Oh?" Vas stood in the full brunt of the candlelight, letting its warm, flickering flame reveal his features. When their eyes met, a stillness settled over him. His muscles relaxed. A familiar warmth swirled in his chest, reminding him of the night he met Anastasia. *Did the sisters share some sort of magic? Is this what it felt like to be near a flame mage of Haven?* He couldn't pull away from her gaze.

Pink flushed across Lana's cheeks, and she turned her head aside.

He wondered what she was thinking. *What had she meant?* But he couldn't form words, still caught in the same restful silence of her proximity.

Lana stepped closer to him, inspecting the horns that curled from just behind his temples, around his ears and pointed into a dull tip below his earlobe. His hair was messy and curled in soft, pale ringlets. His skin was a deep, smoky color that contrasted against his silvery hair. Vas was the monotone of a moonlit night, except for his eyes. His eyes were bright, wild green.

"What?" he asked, nervousness overtaking his thoughts. *Was she afraid? Did she think he was disgusting—a monster, a freak?*

Lana moved around him in a circle and he turned around with her, never letting her stay at his back for longer than a few moments. She stopped and finally sheathed her sword.

"I guess you're kind of dirty, but not enough to warrant hiding in the corner from me," she said half-heartedly. She reached out, as if to touch his ram-like horn, but let her hand fall away before making contact with him.

"You don't think I'm scary?"

She laughed, smiling at him in such a familiar way it made his heart ache and his head throb as memories flitted in and out of his consciousness. "Scary? No. In need of some clothes that aren't torn to shreds? Yes. I'm sure there's something around the temple."

"I'll find something, then," he said, but didn't move. They stood in front of each other, their eyes locked as silence fell over them. The faintest brush of heat rushed through his veins, like a golden thread twisting in his blood, reminding him again of the first time he'd met Anastasia.

Lana chewed on her lower lip, her eyes shifting to his horns again and to the points of his ears. "Did the magic do this to you? Like Shiloh? Or—" Lana snapped her mouth shut. Embarrassment lit her cheeks red.

This wasn't Anastasia he reminded himself. No matter how much she looked like her, sounded like her, even acted like her. This was her sister. He steeled himself against his aching heart and crossed his arms, shaking his head so that his hair fell over his eyes. "I'm half-Brynian. Nothing happened. I was born this way. So, anyway, is Anastasia with you?"

"Brynian." She turned the word over in her mouth. "I don't know what that is, but what's new?" Almost as an after-thought, she added, "Anastasia is...not with me. It's compli-cated. "

She was incomprehensible. How sheltered was she that she had no clue about the world beyond Haven? He'd never known that Anastasia had a sister. Royal lineages of the near-by kingdoms—even Haven—was something he'd studied. *Lana.* With that thought, another jolt of pain shot through his head, and Vas pressed the palm of his hand to his forehead.

"What's wrong?"

"I don't know." Just as quickly as it had come, the pain dissipated. "Headache. It's been a long day."

Lana laughed without any real mirth. "Yeah. Same."

He dropped his hands and looked at her through the fringe of his moonlight curls.

She met his gaze and offered a smile. "So, I guess, you'll head out for home in the morning."

"I guess so, but I have no idea how to get there." He knew he was now closer to the western side of the desert. "Is there a dock on this side of the desert? Or someway to get back to the mainland nearby?"

"I dunno," Lana said with a shrug that made the melted wax slosh down the sides of the candle she still held. "I wish I could help, but I don't know how to get anywhere."

He dropped his eyes and sighed, crestfallen. Before the accident, he'd arrived to the desert on the southern side, taking the port from Seai. If there was no dock on the west side, he'd end up too far away from the safety of the temple when night fell. The Hollows would surely catch him.

Lana shifted from foot to foot. "Uh, well, maybe Shiloh can help."

He pushed his hair from his face, but kept staring at his feet. "Your companion? Isn't he asleep or something?"

"Well, sure, probably. We'll deal with it in the morning." She turned and started off toward the sanctuary.

Vas didn't follow.

Lana stopped in the door and looked back at him. Light from the sanctuary shone at her back, making a halo around her body of flickering gold. "Are you coming?"

"I'm fine here." Even in the enormous room of the sanctuary, he would feel like an outsider. He didn't belong there with them. He fiddled nervously with his elbow, glancing between Lana and the shadows of the nearly empty room he still stood in.

She shrugged. "Suit yourself. It's warmer in here. The skeletons aren't nearly that creepy once you get used to them." She slipped back into the sanctuary and put the candle she'd been carrying back on its pedestal.

Vas sighed. It didn't matter where he slept in the temple. Whether he slept in the shadows of this statue room or in the Hall of the Fallen Warriors, he would still be a Brynian among Havenites. Loneliness clouded his thoughts. For just one night, he didn't want to sleep in an empty room. Or perhaps he just didn't want to be in a room without her. He brushed away the passing thought. It was Anastasia he wanted to see again, not her sister, he reminded himself.

He took one last glance at the door that led out to the desert. In the darkness, rolling across the dunes, the Hollow horde ran straight for them. Their bodies undulated as they made their way across the sand. Vas stood frozen, watching the horror that would soon be upon them.

CHAPTER 15

Lana

They'd found her. Her heart hammered against her chest as she fought to breathe. The creatures were coming. The desert wind rushed into the room, bringing with it the tell-tale stench of death that always rode the breeze around the monsters.

"You said they can't come in here, right?" Vas asked. He jerked his head, looking back and forth between the approaching horde and Lana's terrified expression. "Right?" he repeated.

Lana nodded. That's what Shiloh had said. She'd felt so safe here, even in the shadows. How stupid had she been? Her nightmares would never let her be safe.

Howls ripped through the night, shattering the air. The monsters were close. She could see the smoky magic wrapping around their canine bodies. Red sparks jumped from creature to creature, magic sizzling the air. It was over. She was as good as dead.

"We need to hide," Vas said, taking her wrist gently in his hand, though his voice was hard with urgency. "Come with me." He pulled her, but she couldn't move. Her legs were locked and her body heavy with fear.

Why had she ever thought she could do anything? She couldn't help Shiloh. She couldn't find her mom in this horrible nightmare world. She'd only die trying.

"I can carry you. Let me carry you," Vas said, words tumbling from his lips like a rushing waterfall as he wrapped an arm around her waist.

Lana nodded, but they were too late. The monsters rushed up the stairs, mouths frothing with delight. Their red eyes locked on them. There was no where to hide from that stare.

Vas pulled her into his arms and rushed backwards towards the light of the sanctuary as the Hollows threw themselves at the open doors of the temple.

Thud. Thud. Thud.

The monsters crashed against an invisible barrier that sparked with golden light, just like it had back home in the yard. Their bodies fell to the ground in piles, while others climbed over, desperate to get in.

But they couldn't.

Lana sighed as relief washed over her and relaxed against Vas. "They can't get in," she said.

"They can't get in," Vas repeated.

The Hollows cried out as their attempts were thwarted at every turn by the sparks of golden light.

"We're safe," Lana said, taking a shuddering breath. Safe, but useless. What use could she be? If she froze in the face of danger, how did she expect to find her mom? And if the Hollows had gotten in, she'd be dead by now.

"Let's go into the light," Vas whispered, pulling away from Lana and guiding her towards the sanctuary.

Lana didn't resist and followed silently as she tried to ignore the frenzy of monsters just outside the temple doors.

CHAPTER 16

Lana

Upon entering the sanctuary, Vas took up a distant corner and seemed to fall immediately asleep. Lana stared at the ceiling for hours, trying to calm her racing heart. Eventually, she started watching Vas curiously from her side of the room. She couldn't help herself. Every time she looked at him, she felt this burning warmth. A whisper in the back of her mind recognized him, knew him. Lana brushed the thought away, rationalizing that maybe it was the way he fidgeted as he talked or the green of his eyes that reminded her of Liam. She bit her bottom lip. Her thoughts shifting between wondering again if Liam was okay and remembering his smile and the way he stood by her, protected her, to intense guilt for bringing him to this place full of danger.

She wanted to help Vas, and not just because his eyes were green like Liam's or because he was adorable, like a lost puppy. Her cheeks heated at her own thoughts, and she reprimanded herself. She couldn't indulge in silly thoughts like that. Besides, it was only because he reminded her of Liam. She needed to focus on finding her mom and the amulet, waking Anastasia to save the world from monsters, and then getting out of this world—safe at home, where things could be as they should be. If she could even do that. Her thoughts turned dark again, remembering how she'd frozen in the face of the Hollows outside. If she wanted to save anyone, let alone help Vas get home, she needed to face her fears.

Words bubbled up from that foreign warmth in her chest—*my prince*—but those two words were full of sorrow, grief. Lana pressed her fingers against her eyebrows, breathing through the weight of emotions she didn't recognize. *Why was she so sad?*

She exhaled roughly, trying to force her brain into stillness. Stubbornness and force were Lana's specialty when it came to ignoring the moving of her mind, so with some effort, she shoved the thoughts of Vas, the strange sorrow, and the insurmountable task ahead into a tidy box and threw it in the back of her mind where all the other nonsense lived. One day at a time. One task at a time.

Worries were for tomorrow. She closed her eyes, focusing on the sound of wind outside the temple, and eventually fell asleep.

Warmth, like a radiant golden sun, pulled Lana. Her body soared through space, like she was in a car driving too fast, watching flashes of images and emotion that burst and faded.

When the world stilled, Lana found herself in a room with a long table down the center, surrounded by familiar figures—the general from her recent nightmare, her father, and Shiloh. As she glanced around, she knew with a dream-like knowledge that she was in the city hall of Haven and that her long-dead father was once the head of Haven—Commander Creon.

"They've come for the captured Hollow," General Alix Bludeg said. "You must let her go."

"It's already gone," Shiloh said. He looked different. Younger, softer. His hair wasn't the mystical purple that Lana remembered it being, but instead a delicate gray.

"She's gone?" Alix's eyes widened with a breathless panic as her hands fisted on the table.

Screams rose from the streets below.

"We don't have time for this! The Hollows have come," Lana felt herself saying. Her mind reeled momentarily before she realized the reality—Anastasia's memories were playing out in her dreams. "Our people are terrorized below by the beasts! Does no one else care for our people, or the Silvids? We are the only ones who can protect them." Anastasia steeled herself while heading to the door, spurred on by the Hollows' screeching.

"The soldiers are already fighting in the city, Anastasia, but we are still overrun. We must consider other options," her father, Commander Creon, said.

Before anyone could stop her, Anastasia ran through the doors and burst out on the street, her sword blazing with the power of the flame. Alix ran after her, bloodlust in her own eyes. The pair raced after the beasts. Anastasia moved with desperation as she tried to keep her people from harm, but it was a bloodbath. The streets of Haven ran red.

Hours passed as Anastasia fought alongside the general and the Haven soldiers. Her fiery sword spilled putrid blood and gore all over Haven, but their attempts were in vain.

Her father was right.

Haven had fallen.

Lana tried to pull away, to shut her consciousness from the images, but Anastasia's golden presence forced her to stay and watch. There was still something important she wanted Lana to know.

Time passed, swirled, stilled. Anastasia stood in the center of an ornate room. Her father and Shiloh stood beside her.

"There's nothing else we can do," her father said. "We have to evacuate the remaining people."

"There's nowhere safe on this continent," Shiloh said.

"Shiloh," her father said in an almost reprimand. "Do you think I've had you studying our ancestral land for nothing? I want you to open the Great Gate."

Anastasia glared at her father. "We'll be leaving the Silvids defenseless! We can't just abandon them."

"Why not? What good have any of the fae ever done for us?" Creon asked, his chest puffed out and chin held high.

Anastasia straightened, making the emblem of Haven clear on her tunic. She was raised to be a warrior to fight for her people. Why did he expect her to back down now? "We have a duty to protect them because we are the only ones who can. The Hollows will destroy them all if we let them run free. Our magic is the only thing that evens the fight."

"We need to worry about *our* people," he said. "If you were in charge, you would understand."

Anastasia breathed hard through her nose, a frustrated huff, and turned her attention to Shiloh. "You can't do this."

"He must." Her father put himself between Anastasia and Shiloh.

"Shiloh," she pleaded.

He dropped his head. "I don't know any alternatives. The Hollows have grown too large for even us to handle. We've lost too many warriors."

"We've relied on the generals and their knights sent from the Silvid Court for too long. Bludeg and Meredith were good soldiers, but they cannot keep our people from dying. Especially now that even Meredith is lost to the Hollows." Commander Creon looked down at his daughter with a defeated expression. "There's nothing left to do and not enough blessed with a gift as great as yours to do anything."

"I can do something. I will do something." Anastasia clenched her fists.

"There's nothing you can do," her father said.

Shiloh forced a blank expression and turned away, looking anywhere but at Anastasia.

"There is something, isn't there?" Anastasia pushed past her father to stand directly in front of Shiloh.

He just shook his head, refusing to meet her gaze.

"What is it? Shiloh, tell me."

Shiloh bit his lip and stared at the ground. "Nothing that would help anyone."

"Lies!" She turned suddenly toward her father. "You know something about this! What are you two hiding?"

Her father frowned. "Stop with this nonsense."

"Fine," she said. "Then I'm just going to go out and fight them now. Either I'll kill them all or die trying."

"Wait!" Shiloh reached out and delicately grabbed her arm. "Don't."

"I have to do something. You two are both selfish cowards. I won't let an entire race be devoured simply to save myself." Anastasia jerked from Shiloh's loose grip.

Her father sighed and gave a meaningful look to Shiloh. "You called me cold for proposing my solution, but you see what yours would lead to."

"What?" Anastasia looked between the pair of them.

"He wants to experiment on you." Shiloh glared at the floor, not daring to look up at her father.

"It's not an experiment if I know it will work." Her father sighed. "This is what Keepers are born to do, Shiloh. This is her nature and why she is Keeper of the Light. You may think of me however you like, but sacrifice is necessary at times."

"What are you talking about?" Anastasia's heart thumped against her ribs, anticipation drawing the seconds out unbearably.

"The sunlight matrix," Shiloh said, "can be the foundation for stronger spells. Longer spells." He let that sink in before continuing. "Your father," he spat the word, his face growing red—Anastasia had never seen him so angry or upset—as he continued, still staring at the ground, "wants to use you as the conduit of a sunlight matrix to erect a wall that will keep the Hollows imprisoned in the desert, while the rest of us escape through the Great Gate. By putting you into a state of in-betweens, I'll be able to open a Great Gate relatively easily and for a much longer time, allowing more Havenites to escape Kaelum. You will not know death. You will not know life. He wants to make you a living statue."

"The warden of the Hollows and protector of the Silvids," her father said. "She will be the foundation that keeps those monsters trapped here, and the savior who sets us free."

"It's ridiculous," Shiloh said through clenched teeth. "You can't expect her to do that. If you want the gate open longer, we can find another way or you can sacrifice yourself!"

Creon turned on Shiloh with a scowl and bared teeth. "You don't think I would if I could? I don't have enough magic to trigger the stasis, let alone maintain it long enough to save the Havenites." He turned towards Anastasia, eyes rimmed with unshed tears. "I'd readily give my very soul to spare my daughter from pain."

The tears in her father's eyes washed away what little fear she had. "I'll do it," Anastasia said. "I would gladly sacrifice myself to save them." Her heart ached for a moment as she thought of the one person she wished she could have saved—the Silvid prince. Though she met him only once, news of his death in the desert had shattered her.

The room fell silent. Shiloh stared at her with wide eyes brimming with tears.

"I'll leave you to the preparations." Her father looked back at Anastasia. "Your mother will assist Shiloh with this spellwork. I must attend to our people." He hesitated for a moment, staring at her.

She felt the weight of his gaze, full of words he wouldn't say.

"Are you coming back?" Shiloh asked.

"I can't." Her father stood at the door with his back to them.

"But—" Shiloh moved to speak, but Anastasia put her hand on Shiloh's arm and gave him a look that caught his words in his throat.

"This is who we are. This was her decision. I am respecting it, as you should mine." Then Creon left.

"It's all right, Shi."

Shiloh's face closed and hardened. In silence, he gathered the instruments he required, shoving them in a bag that he slung across his shoulder, and moved to the door. Anastasia followed. He led her through the city and to the spiraling stairs that led to the western temple.

Though she wanted to, Anastasia didn't question him as they climbed the stairs to the temple. In pained silence, he led her to the Hall of Fallen Warriors. The room was lined with caskets, beautiful glass art made by the artisans of Haven, whose magical skills were delicate enough to work such fragile material. Anastasia kept her eyes away from the dead. She didn't want to see familiar faces in this hall. Though she didn't look, her heart felt heavy.

The front of the room differed from how she last remembered it. An empty coffin was opened and displayed there.

"Your father already had this set up. He planned to sacrifice you for his gate from the beginning," Shiloh said, breaking the silence. He dropped his bag on the floor by the coffin without care, glaring at the place she would soon rest.

"I chose this to help the Silvids," she said. "With my last breath, I will always choose to help them."

"Sure. I should have expected you to be so idiotically self-sacrificial. You always have been." He sighed and swiped the back of his hand across his eyes. "But without this, opening a Great Gate for such an extended time would be almost impossible. Ripping and sustaining a hole between worlds large enough for all the Haven people to escape requires a strong in-between, and now you will exist perpetually between life and death. I'll be able to open a gate for him at his beck and call. You think that's a coincidence? He must have something planned. There has to be another way to do this and to help the Silvids too."

"My father is not a conniving strategist, like you seem to think." Anastasia paused, thinking briefly of her mother, who was much more cunning than her father. "Maybe there is another way, but we don't have time to find it."

"We would have time if he would just let me look where I wanted to. If he would just give me access to the full library, instead of just the books he wanted me to read. If we could just— If I could—"

Anastasia stopped him, wrapping her arms around him. "It's okay, Shi."

He buried his face against her shoulder and sobbed. She held him like that for a long time until his tears subsided. When they pulled away, Anastasia saw her mother standing in the corner, looking pensive.

At the sight of her mother, Lana snapped to the surface again. *Elaine.* A bit younger than Lana remembered, but still, that was her mother. *Their* mother. Lana struggled with the overwhelming evidence that Kaelum was her true family home, that Anastasia was her sister—right now, the only family she still had. She couldn't leave Kaelum without Anastasia. She couldn't abandon her, like their father had. In that moment, Lana decided to take Anastasia with her. Once they found their mother and saved Kaelum, they could be together again. Only Lana didn't know how to accomplish any of that.

Her mother pushed away from the corner and approached Shiloh and Anastasia.

"Elaine." Shiloh nodded toward her.

"You know what we must do, Shiloh." She stared at him intensely.

He returned her gaze. They stared at each other for a long moment, exchanging some meaningful communication that Anastasia couldn't understand.

"What do you need me to do?" Anastasia asked.

Her mother stood in front of Anastasia and brushed a loose strand of hair from her face. "There is a tunic in the other room that I've already inscribed with sigils for this spell. Go change. We'll get the room ready."

Anastasia obeyed. She heard them whisper fervently as she left, but she ignored them. If Shiloh was right, that her father wanted to do this spell for the gate, then would it even work to keep the Silvids safe? She ran her fingers across her eyes slowly, pushing away the beginnings of a headache.

In the room, a traditional white and gold tunic was draped across a chair. She pulled off her armor and set it on a table nearby, and quickly pulled on the shirt. It exposed her arms and neck, but covered her entirely otherwise, falling in a long sheet of fabric to her mid-thigh.

Despite knowing she would be unconscious and inert, she kept her sword strapped across her hips. Somehow, she knew that she wouldn't be inert forever, and when she woke, she wanted to be prepared.

She entered the Hall of the Fallen Warriors, and they both fell silent again.

"What do we do if this doesn't work?" Anastasia crossed her arms and stared them both down.

"It will work. Your mother and I are doing the spellwork, after all. The remaining Havenites will escape and the wall will go up to keep the Hollows in the desert," Shiloh said bitterly.

"And if the wall fails?" Anastasia asked.

Her mother held up her hand for Shiloh to remain quiet. "Unlike your father, there are many among us who do not wish to see the death of the Silvids. If the wall does not hold, then I will find a way to keep them safe. Even after we leave Haven, I intend to keep contact with the Silvid Court royals."

Anastasia furrowed her brows. "But, Mom. You don't have the flames. What could you do against the Hollows?" Her mother had small traces of magic, but not fire. Elaine's arms were tattooed with sigils and twisting script, allowing her to harness more magic than she innately had. Elaine's magic was different. It was the magic of souls.

"Just trust me," she said with a soft smile. She held her hand out for Anastasia, and she came to the familiar gesture, grasping her mother's arm against her own.

Shiloh watched the pair with a blank expression.

Elaine led Anastasia down to the coffin and helped her step inside. Anastasia laid down, hesitantly. Her mother nodded and moved the pillows and arranged the sparse interior for her daughter to get comfortable. Then, she took the chalk that was often used for magic wards and painted symbols across Anastasia's throat and arms.

Anastasia closed her eyes. Soon, Shiloh and her mother's chanting filled the room. The rush of magic wasn't an unpleasant feeling. Warmth wrapped around her and settled into her bones, weighing her down until she felt rooted to the spot.

The chanting changed rhythm, and suddenly she wasn't heavy anymore. Anastasia opened her eyes and saw that she was looking down at her own body. Her mother dangled a necklace in her hand and a jar. She dumped the jar of desert sand onto Anastasia's body and a blue flash that reminded her of the wellspring water erupted in a rush of sparks before settling down into Anastasia's body.

Then Anastasia was pulled, drawn down from her place in the air above her body, into the necklace, which Lana recognized as the pendant that her mother always wore. Anastasia shuddered. She was within the pendant now, trapped in frigid glass.

The flames at the edge of Shiloh's circle died down and disappeared. Their chanting faded away.

"It's done," her mother said.

"Once this is over, how are we going to wake her up?" Shiloh asked.

Her mother held the necklace up high. "You leave that to me. I will make a new home for my daughter, where she can live away from all of this."

Shiloh furrowed his brows. "If you are suggesting what I think you are, then you're insane. A changeling? She won't be the same. She won't know us."

Her mother smiled, but there was a furtive darkness burning in her gaze. Another secret. "She will know me. If you love her, you'll let her live however I bring her back."

"And what about what she wants? What about the Silvids?" Shiloh shoved up from the stone, shaking with the tide of his emotions.

"I have a plan for that. I don't want to see them die either, but I can't stop them all from death." Elaine settled the amulet over her head, letting it fall across her chest heavily.

"And what's your plan, then?" Shiloh wrapped his arms around himself, as he turned away from Elaine.

Her mother considered for a moment. "Might as well tell you, I suppose. Maybe you can be of help to me." She patted the necklace, tracing a finger over the gem.

Anastasia curled up in the depths of the scarlet glass and watched in silence. She was tired. Too tired to understand what was being said, what she felt or what to do or what they had done.

"I'm going to make a home for them in the ancestral land," she said.

"There's no way they could survive there. I've read all the books about our lands." Shiloh paced, his slow steps echoing in the room.

"Have you ever been there?" her mother asked.

"Well, no."

"The fae will have their ways of surviving. Other courts live more closely intertwined with the human world. I'll seek contact with those courts for aid. Beyond that, if finding a new home is their only chance at survival, I'm sure they will make it work." Elaine shrugged, tucking a stray lock of hair behind her ear. "And if that doesn't work, I have a communication mirror set up with Harmoni and Theoden. We will find another way."

Shiloh sighed. "You should have talked to Anastasia about this. She's not going to like this. Maybe we should reverse this now." He stopped in front of the coffin, staring down at Anastasia's lifeless body.

Her mother frowned. "Anastasia wanted this. Yes, the wall has no hope of working. I told Creon that, but this is our best chance to save us all and delay the Hollows' conquest. We'll all start over. Come with us and help me."

Shiloh shook his head. "I'm not leaving her here."

Her mother sighed, exasperated, pushing off the coffin to stand. "Fine. Stay with my daughter's empty shell, if that's what you desire." Then, she turned to leave.

Shiloh's eyes never wavered from Anastasia's body. "I'll find a way to make this right again. I promise."

From the dark of the amulet, Anastasia watched as Shiloh's figure grew smaller with her mother's retreat—a young man, alone, surrounded by skeletons.

CHAPTER 17

Shiloh

L ong before the first rays of dawn descended on the temple, Shiloh woke. His first thoughts drifted to Luze. *Had he made it to Haven safe, even with two bodies in tow?* Maybe he should have gone with him, put all three unconscious people on the sled and taken them down the water elevator, but Shiloh hated that elevator. He didn't trust it. When the Silvids in the temple were the ones running the thing, it was bearable—they had magic to manipulate the water for worst-case scenarios, even if they were hesitant to use it.

The temple seemed so quiet without Luze, so cold. Shiloh frowned. He should be considering more important things—like Elaine's knotted web of magic on Anastasia and Lana. Tightening the blanket around his shoulders, Shiloh sat up from his haphazard nest. His eyes weren't yet adjusted to the dim of the early morning, so he sat in silence, letting his mind wander.

Anastasia. He'd been so certain that Elaine had taken her soul and created a changeling—a fae soul in a mundane body. But if that had been the case, why hadn't Anastasia woken? When the soul re-entered Anastasia's body from Lana, she should have woken with her memories. *Could Lana truly be Anastasia's sister? Or had the spells gone awry and split her soul somehow?* Still clutching the blanket around himself, he tapped his fingers on the fabric in a contemplative rhythm. Frustration made his skin itch and he wanted to scream. He needed Elaine, or at least her books. He could fix this if only he knew how. Elaine wasn't the only one who could harness soul sigils, he thought as he glared at the floor.

Shiloh hunched over, picking at the skin of his lower lip, his eyes unfocused. Nothing was unfolding correctly. If those Hollows hadn't appeared at Lana's house, he wouldn't have brought Lana to Kaelum so soon. *How had they managed to get through to the mundane world in the first place? Better yet, why?* He wanted to talk to Luze. Surely he would be able to make sense of this. Lana was lucky he'd been watching. If he hadn't been considering the possibility that she might be the key, she'd be dead by now. But she wasn't the easy solution to Anastasia's curse—or at least not the entire solution.

Elaine had all the answers, but she wouldn't talk to him and had so many wards up, Luze could never locate her for long. He made a habit of checking Elaine's house in Haven at least once a month, but never got any closer to unraveling the magic on Anastasia.

He missed Anastasia. He needed her. Shiloh didn't know how to live in a world where she didn't. *Foolish*, said a familiar voice from the recesses of his mind.

"Go away. Go away. Go away," Shiloh muttered underneath his breath. He hated the Voice.

Forget the girl. She won't love you. The Voice faded, too weak to continue the comments that Shiloh knew would surface if he let it.

"I can't," he whispered, burying his face against the blanket. He couldn't let her go. Memories flickered through his mind—the flood, his parents, her. He forced his mind away from those dark thoughts.

Anastasia saved him, stayed by him when everyone else just gave him glances full of pity. She was the one to encourage him to study magic, after passing the Flame's Trial when they were young. Without her, he would have been alone.

She was his only friend and he was hers—at least, until the Hollow War brought those obnoxious Silvids to Haven. He sneered at the memory. Ever since Alix and Meredith showed up, Anastasia had less time for him. She was too busy training, fighting, she said, but he'd seen her with them.

He would show her. When he broke this spell on her, she would finally see him. He would save her this time. Life could go back to the way it was before the Hollows ever appeared.

Shiloh stood, stretching his sore muscles. After opening a gate in the middle of Elaine's wards and feeding his magic into the temple, his body ached. The temple was always the worst of it, because it wasn't the kind of magic he was used to—all his life, he'd only ever used sigil magic, which didn't ever seem to drain him. Even opening the gate was more mentally taxing than anything, considering the sigils on Anastasia's body did the heavy lifting, pulling magic into the spell from the desert. But feeding the temple wards was more like battle magic—intuitive and raw, tugging at the flame within him.

Battle magic excited him as much as it terrified him. Summoning the flame was as natural as breathing, but the more he used that magic, the louder the Voice became. With each blissful flame that he summoned he felt closer to a precipice, closer to losing control. The flames would consume him. He knew magic was dangerous—use too much and the mage burns from the inside out as the soul consumes itself to burn.

He could use that magic, but he hoped he wouldn't have to.

You will have to. The words were barely a breath in his mind, but the Voice repeated its insidious whisper.

Shiloh did his best to ignore it, clenching his hands in the blanket. It was just fear, he reassured himself, pushing it away. The Voice's faint laughter disappeared until Shiloh was alone in his mind again.

Sunrise drew near. He should prepare for their descent into Haven. As he looked around the dim sanctuary, a pair of bright-green eyes looked back.

Shiloh flinched, surprised by the unexpected intruder. He looked familiar. White hair, gray skin, green eyes, and... Shiloh's eyes widened as he saw the horns. *Prince Vasileios of the Silvid Court.* But he was dead—no, suspended in the wellspring. *Could he be mistaken?* He'd only met the prince once, in passing, and the prince always wore a hood, despite the fact that everyone knew about his horns. Shiloh always thought it strange, considering beast traits symbolized power in the Wild Court of Brynia.

"How?" Shiloh asked into the empty silence.

"Good morning," Vas whispered. "I have a favor to ask."

"A favor?" Shiloh scoffed and turned toward a side room. "Come on then. Let's leave the girl to sleep. We can speak in here." He gestured for Vas to follow. *The girl.* Shiloh couldn't bear to say Anastasia's name when she wasn't truly awake in her own body, but calling the name of her sister—if she really was her sister—seemed wrong too.

Shiloh led him into a small room—barely more than a storage closet, to be truthful. It was where he'd been keeping extra supplies. He figured he might as well prepare for their descent to Haven while dealing with the prince.

Vas stood by the door, watching as Shiloh rifled through the cabinets.

"What is it you want?" Shiloh asked.

"I want to go home. I was hoping you might know how to get to the mainland. Can you help me?" Vas crossed his arms, looking away to the corner of the room.

Shiloh pulled a bag from underneath a shelf and shook it out. They wouldn't need much. The walk from the entrance to the fountain would take them a day or two, shorter if Luze met them at the outpost. He grimaced and piled the rations of dried fruits, beans, and crackers into the bag, wishing the desert had more to offer than what little he could forage in the lush cavern of Haven and cultivate in one of the gardens that were littered across Haven and what he managed to steal from the mundane world through portals. Not that he'd be able to access the mundane world anymore, losing one easy source of food.

"Can you help?" Vas repeated.

Shiloh sighed and tied the bag closed. "I'll tell you the way, but that's the end of it." He didn't want anything to do with the prince. Even seeing him now was enough to make his stomach knot. It had been over twenty years, but even in all that time, Shiloh couldn't banish the memory of the prince's hands on Anastasia. The way they had danced together, laughed. She'd looked so happy, so free. Shiloh had never seen her like that. He wanted to be the one to make her smile, not some prince who probably danced with a new girl every night. She deserved better. "Go through Haven. In the north, there is another exit that leads to a protected port. Though I make no guarantee, there should be boats there."

"Is the port not being used anymore? Has the mainland given up on the desert?" Vas readjusted his crossed arms, once, twice, and then let them fall to his side.

Shiloh laughed. "Given up? Oh, you have missed so much while you've been floating in the wellspring. I do wonder how you managed to crawl out. Nothing has been able to leave or enter this island in twenty-five years. I've told you what you need to know—now leave."

"Aren't you going down to Haven?"

"Not with you. You are a liability. If something happens to you, whatever royal fae are left would blame me." Shiloh slung the bag over his shoulders and shifted to another cabinet, pulling out several full canteens of water from the underground river. He planned to take everything he'd been storing back to the apartment. He didn't have any need to come back to the temple now that Anastasia wasn't tied to the spell wall.

Vas stared in silence, lips pursed in thought. "My parents wouldn't blame someone who tried to help."

"Your parents?" Shiloh bit his lips together, holding his words in. The king and queen of Silvis were gone, and Shiloh didn't really care what the royals thought. It wasn't like they would even know something had happened to the prince. Everyone thought he was dead. No. He just didn't want this pretty boy prince around Anastasia. He'd seen them together the night of the prince's debut. The way they danced. The look in Anastasia's eyes. He couldn't bear the sight of them together. The prince would steal her away, like those two fae knights had during the war.

Even so, Shiloh couldn't tell the prince, no matter how much he disliked him, about his parents. He knew what it was like to be alone in the world. He wouldn't be the one to break that news. Perhaps it was cruel of him to keep the knowledge to himself. Selfish to refuse for the sake of his own pain, his own past.

Shiloh shook his head. He wouldn't let the prince accompany them. He couldn't. "Moreover, I don't trust you."

"What? Why?" Vas held his hands out, palm up, confusion clear on his face.

"Why should I? The prince is dead and now you show up, looking just like him? No. If you travel with us, you'll kill us both," he said, though he didn't actually believe it to be true. Magic, especially pure magic like the wellspring, was fickle. He had no idea how the prince had awoken and escaped the wellspring, but it was the most logical response. Brynians had magic that could create illusions, but none so perfect or complex as replicating another fae—that was the kind of magic only found in myths. However, it was the perfect excuse. Shiloh held back a sinister grin. He would not let the prince anywhere near Anastasia.

"Are you serious?" Vas threw his hands up in the air for a moment before ruffling his hands through his hair. "Who would even want to kill you? Why?"

"You can't come with us," Shiloh said. The words hung in the air with a sense of comforting finality. Once the prince left, Shiloh would wait an hour or so before taking Anastasia into Haven. If they hurried, they could be at the apartment before nightfall. She would be safe there and he could begin figuring out how to unravel Elaine's magic. Everything would return to the way it was meant to be.

CHAPTER 18

Lana

Lana woke in the early hours of the morning with words playing like broken record in her head.

We're the only ones that can. We're the only ones. only ones. We.

She took a deep breath, trying to compose herself after the strange dream. No, not a dream, but memory. Anastasia had shown her those memories for a reason.

What was Anastasia trying to tell her? Those words must have been hers. What did she mean *We're the only one that can?* Can what? She pressed her fingers against her eyelids, replaying the memories in her mind. Anastasia wanted nothing more than to save the fae from the Hollows, but she said *we.* No, Lana thought, she couldn't do anything. She wasn't brave enough.

We. That word repeated in her mind, echoing around the empty darkness of her thoughts, until it hit her. Together. If she could connect with Anastasia like Shiloh said, then perhaps she could help them. Perhaps she could wake Anastasia, find her mom, save the fae and return home with Liam somehow. She just needed to try harder. Lana reached inside herself, searching for some remnants of Anastasia in her own consciousness, but found nothing. It may take time, but hope once again fluttered in Lana's chest.

Dawn was slowly breaking; soon the sun would rise high over the horizon and fill the desert outside the temple with heat. Her body ached from lying on the floor. Her stomach growled, gnawing at itself. Lana had never felt such intense hunger before.

She pushed herself up to a sitting position. The candles had gone out. Luckily, stained-glass windows near the ceiling let in thin streams of colored light, so she could see the room. She was alone. Shiloh's folded blankets were empty and Vas was nowhere to be seen.

Lana held her breath, straining to hear anything that might indicate where they were. The temple didn't seem very big, so there weren't exactly many places to search. Lana started with the main entryway. The room was quiet. Dim light trickled in from the open doorway, which no longer sparkled with golden light. With a quick search, she realized this room was empty.

Remembering the memories in her dream, she slipped through the sanctum of the dead and into the side room where Anastasia had left her armor. It was there, draped across a stone bench and untouched. A layer of dust covered the metal. Something—Anastasia, perhaps—compelled her to reach for the comfort of the delicate armor—a leather cuirass with a chainmail tasset and collar. Anastasia wore this every day—as a symbol of her duty as Keeper. Anastasia had been fond of it. Lana ran her finger across the metal, surprised she knew pieces of Anastasia's life.

Lana brushed away the dust before sliding the armor onto her body, putting on the clothes that Anastasia had worn so long ago. Somehow, they were perfect, untouched by time—other than the dust that was irritating Lana's nose. Leather, cloth, and metal mesh fit against her, and she felt comforted, safe. With the sword strapped to her side, Lana felt transformed.

She still needed to find Vas and Shiloh, so she returned to the sanctuary, giving one last look around before she turned toward the doors at the back. As she neared them, she noticed the doors were ajar. Hushed voices floated from the hallway beyond.

"You can't come with us," Shiloh said.

"But..." Vas paused.

"I cannot allow it," said Shiloh.

Lana pushed the door open, letting the early morning light sift into the hallway. "And why not?"

"How long have you been listening?" Shiloh's eyes widened as they landed on her, fully clothed like a Haven warrior.

"Why can't he come with us?"

Shiloh looked from Vas to Lana. "Because." He took a deep breath. "We cannot trust him. He is...Brynian."

"And?" Lana asked.

"I have no need to explain politics." Shiloh cut his eyes over to Vas, something unsaid in his gaze.

Vas scoffed. "He thinks I'm a spy."

"A spy?" Shiloh laughed coldly. "What need do Hollows have for spies? I think you're an assassin. With only two humans left who can stand against those creatures, I'm certain your beast queen would love to dispose of us."

"What are you talking about? Beast queen?" Vas furrowed his brows.

"Acting as if you don't know? Wretch. You will not accompany us." Shiloh, with two bags tied across his back, pushed toward the door.

"I don't care about your baseless assumptions. I'm not going without him." Lana crossed her arms and looked over at Vas. She didn't really understand why she was putting herself in the middle of this argument. Shiloh could be right. He'd saved her once before, but her heart ached at the thought of leaving Vas. She wanted to help him, wanted him to stay with them.

"You don't even know him!" Shiloh raised his hands in frustration.

"I don't even know you!" she retorted.

"You know me better than him." Shiloh stabbed his finger toward Vas.

Vas stood, a hopeless frown on his face. "I promise, I won't hurt you—either of you. Please. Trying for the southern dock would be suicide and heading through Haven alone I'll most certainly get lost and never find my way out of those caves. Let me travel with you at least until I find another guide in Haven."

"Another guide?" Shiloh scoffed. "There is no one else."

"What?" Vas asked, stiffening with confusion.

"Haven was abandoned decades ago."

Vas's pleading wrapped around Lana's heart and tugged. She couldn't possibly leave him here alone. He needed her. "He's coming with us, or I'm not going."

"And if he kills us? If he tries? What then?" Shiloh tightened his grip on one of the straps across his shoulder.

Lana frowned. Vas wouldn't hurt her. She knew that with a certainty she couldn't explain. "I won't abandon him," Lana said.

"Then you'd sacrifice our safety for his?" Shiloh asked.

"I know he won't hurt us," she said.

"I won't risk your safety," Shiloh said pointedly.

"That settles it," Lana said. "I'll go out in the desert with him then."

Shiloh's jaw slackened as he looked toward her. "What kind of idiotic..." he trailed off in a huff of annoyed noises.

A loud crash echoed from one of the other rooms.

Shiloh's head jolted up, and he glared at Vas. "What have you done?"

"I didn't do anything!" Vas stepped back with his hands up.

Lana turned and rushed toward the other room. She slid to a halt at the door. The sun had barely broken the horizon, leaving the room in dim light and deep shadows. The stained-glass window on the far side of the room was shattered. Specks of colored glass littered the floor.

In the middle of the shards, a Hollow stood on all fours with burnt skin from where the sunlight had touched. Its hulking body was humanoid, but broken and twisted out of shape, into something more like a large wolf. It was a creature of magic, smoke, and bone. Red vines undulated around its form, twisting in and out of sight beyond the shadow of it. Its eyes were red and its jaw was slack, revealing a bit of fabric caught on its fangs.

The reek of the creature, like a rotting compost pile, hit Lana's nose, and she backpedaled into the room, slamming up against Shiloh, who had been gaping at the creature as well. All the color was gone from his face, and he whispered quickly.

"Were the candles lit when you woke?"

Lana shook her head. "I don't remember. No. I don't think so."

"We have to leave. Now." Shiloh turned away from the door, where the Hollow still sniffed at the ground, and quietly made his way into the dark depths of the temple.

However, they soon realized, the Hollow was not alone. As they moved through the temple, deeper and deeper through rooms, more glass shattered. The air shivered with the screeches of Hollows.

Lana focused on the sound of her own breath, reminding herself that she could face this. Anastasia was counting on her. She just had to escape with Shiloh and Vas.

They stumbled into another large room, much like the sanctuary, but instead of coffins, the room was entirely empty save one long table running down the center. There were three doors leading away from the room—the one they just entered from and two others that were blocked by the hulking forms of two Hollows—a large, boxy Hollow and a smaller, lithe one.

The creatures jerked their heads toward them, jaws dripping as they stalked forward. But it was at that moment Lana realized the Hollows were focused entirely on Vas. Shiloh must have noticed this as well because he grabbed Lana and began to pull her toward the far side of the room.

The foreign warmth of Anastasia's presence rushed to the surface and she jerked away from him and drew her sword.

"You idiot," Shiloh hissed, keeping his voice as low as possible. "What do you expect to do?"

"I can't abandon him." Together, she and Anastasia wouldn't abandon him.

Just as the Hollows were about to lunge toward Vas, his body billowed out and shifted. It reminded Lana of silly putty or slime, not at all graceful.

Vas groaned, halfway between some giant cat and himself.

Shiloh stifled a laugh that was quickly cut off when Lana threw herself between Vas and the heavy paw of the smaller Hollow that was about to crash down on Vas. The nails scraped metal, and a golden spark of magic erupted from the chainmail tasset that draped across Lana's thigh. The Hollow hissed and fell back, scrambling away from the magic of the Haven armor.

Vas, his body shifting and popping back into place, grabbed Lana's sword from where it fell at her feet. He twisted suddenly and shoved the blade through the larger Hollow's eye as it attempted to latch onto his leg.

The small Hollow howled, and a chorus of screeches replied.

"That doesn't sound good," Lana said through struggled breaths as she tried to right herself. Anastasia's presence was a mere ghost in her mind, quickly fading. The weight of the Hollow's blow had been more than she expected.

Shiloh muttered under his breath, clearly seething with anger, but golden light dripped from him, flowing like lava to puddle on the floor at his feet. Zigzags of flame burned against the floor in a peculiar pattern. Aglow with a sudden surge of magic, Shiloh staggered, then ran toward Lana and Vas.

"Come on," he said, choking on flames that clawed up his throat. "Quickly."

Shiloh latched onto Lana and dragged her through one of the side doors. At each turn, they met against a Hollow, but Shiloh spewed flames, gold magic like bile dripping from his lips and nose. The Hollows turned away, and those brave enough to get closer were subject to the sword that Vas still wielded.

At the end of a long hallway, Shiloh pulled Lana into a small room. Vas stumbled in behind them. A burst of flame engulfed the floor just outside the door as Shiloh closed it.

The room was barely big enough for the three of them and had a hatch in the middle of the floor. Shiloh wiped golden spit from his face and exhaled a haggard breath.

"There's nothing I can do at this point to stop you." Shiloh's eyelids fluttered, as if struggling against their weight. "Even if I forbade you from accompanying us, I have no strength to keep you from it."

The howls got closer again. With one last look toward the door, Shiloh pulled open the hatch, revealing a deep and empty darkness. Shiloh's fingers trembled as he reached into the dark, summoning a tiny, flickering golden light.

Spiraling stone stairs sank into the dark, twisting on itself like a stone fire escape. Shiloh gestured toward the entrance with a look at Vas. "You first. If there are more beasts waiting, I'd rather you get eaten."

Another howl pierced the air, closer than before. "Quickly," Shiloh urged. "The flame will only hold for so long."

Vas slipped into the hatch and started down the stairs. The golden ball of light followed him down. He stopped a few steps down and waited.

"Lana," he said as he gestured to the entrance again.

She obeyed, stopping behind Vas. They all shifted down, letting Shiloh join them on the narrow staircase. Once they were all in the pit, Shiloh placed his hand against the cool stone and the hatch slid shut with a faint golden glow. The clicking of the hatch's lock echoed into the depth of the pit. It was a long way down.

Even in the dark, Lana could hear Shiloh's struggling breaths and clumsy movements behind her. Barely able to speak, Shiloh urged Vas and Lana to descend with impatient grunts and a few words. A small golden light followed him, lighting the steps just enough for them to descend safely.

As she stared into the vast darkness before them, the temperature shifted. A chill breeze ruffled the back of her neck. Lana lifted her gaze and gasped at the sight.

In the distance, a gentle blue light hovered along paths that led to an enormous city. Stone skyscrapers jutted up into the endless dark, lit only by blue lamps. As she stared, she noticed a sad truth about the city. It was in ruins. Hunks of the skyscrapers were crumbled and littered the ground. Broken lamps spilled their contents on the ground. That glowing blue grew and stretched. It was everywhere. Even sparkling on the ceiling, but darkness was everywhere too — in the shadow of the enormous, broken buildings, hidden around narrow alleyways and overgrown gardens. It was a beautiful trap. Every corner could lead to a Hollow, but also her mother. Her mother was down here somewhere amidst the rubble of the city that she'd called her home.

"Almost there." Shiloh's voice wavered from exhaustion, and he took a deep, ragged breath.

The bottom of the stairs was in sight, but Lana suddenly realized Shiloh was no longer directly above them. The tiny golden light that had danced around them in their long descent flickered and suddenly went out.

"Shiloh?" Lana called, but he didn't answer.

Vas stepped down onto the hard ground and turned at the sound of Lana's voice.

Lana, still on the stairs, opened her mouth to call out again, but was hit with the weight of Shiloh's limp body against her. She yelped as her balance swayed. After a moment's struggle, Lana's foot slipped, and she fell.

Her body pitched backward. Instinctively, she wrapped her arms around Shiloh, keeping him from disappearing from her side as they fell together, sliding down the stairs.

"What's wrong?" Vas shouted, rushing back up the stairs toward them.

She wasn't prepared for the collision. Lana and Shiloh thudded into Vas, sending all three of them sprawling onto the floor at the bottom of the stairs, which was cold and damp. Vas took the brunt of the damage, crumpling beneath them both, his shoulder slamming into the ground.

Lana struggled away from him, pulling Shiloh along with her. He was completely unconscious. She groaned with the effort, nursing aches of her own. Luckily, the fall hadn't been far for any of them—only a few stairs, though it had felt like a lot farther in the dark. She didn't dare to imagine what would have happened if he'd fainted higher on the stairs, or they'd tumbled over the railing.

Vas sat up slowly. Lana scanned him, taking stock of his limbs. All still there and intact. His gaze jerked up in a panic, only relaxing when they rested on Lana again.

"Are you okay?" he asked.

"For the most part. Are you?" she replied.

"Jeez," he said with an exhale. "What happened?"

"I don't know." Lana reached out, patting at Shiloh until she found his face. She held her fingers just beneath his nose for a moment, letting his breath wash across her skin. "He's still breathing, but he fainted or something. The light went out and then so did he."

Vas ruffled his hair, wincing at the movement of his shoulder. "He might have pushed his magic too far. I've heard that can happen."

"Then what do we do?"

Vas shrugged. "Just wait, I guess. He'll need rest and probably water or something when he wakes up."

Her eyes adjusted to the dark. The distant blue glow of the cavern city softly illuminated Vas's silhouette. Pulling her attention from him, Lana sighed and turned to the city behind them. Stone skyscrapers jutted from the ground, reaching towards the ceiling covered with twinkling blue moss. Even from this distance, she could see how time had ravaged the city.

Lush cavern vegetation grew across sidewalks and crawled up walls, breaking through stone and glass, which glittered on the ground. A river rushed in the distance, separating them from the city and it's ethereal mosslight.

How long would Shiloh be unconscious?

She didn't want to wait.

In that city, Liam waited for her. Her mother waited for her. She shifted on the cold stone that cut into her palms. Liam had followed her with no hesitation. He was her only friend. Her best friend, but she'd been keeping a secret from him all this time. If she lost him in this dangerous realm of magic and monsters, he'd never know how she felt. Only on the verge of losing him did Lana realize she'd wasted so much time fearing what might happen if she were honest about her heart. When she saw Liam again, she would finally tell him the truth. She would finally confess the feelings she'd been hiding all these years.

CHAPTER 19

Vas

His shoulder stung, but that wasn't the thought that had his mind spinning in circles. He rubbed a hand across his face, scrubbing his eyes. The woman sitting there with him wore the face of his first love, but something else drew him to her. Now he thought he knew what it was.

He played the last few minutes back through his mind. Her fearful yelp had echoed down the stairs and instinct overwhelmed him. He rushed toward her. Their bodies collided. He'd crashed into cold stone, uncaring for his own pain. That's when it happened. At least, he thought he'd felt a strange flicker inside himself, like a stretching of his very soul. A tethering. He shook his head. Perhaps he was mistaken.

When he was a child, his mother often told him stories. Most often she told him of the moment she'd met his father, or rather the moment she knew that Theoden of Brynia would be the man she married.

"It's a special, quiet kind of magic," she had said. "When the stars fall and we're given our perfect pair. Our fated mate. It takes time to form, but when the thread finally takes shape, you'll have found your person."

"What does it feel like?" Vas had asked. He'd always wished for a love like his parents. The kind that yearns, supports, learns, and grows. A life filled with laughter and partnership, even through grief and change. He'd wanted to fall in love like that. When he met Anastasia, he had been certain that the bond would form between them. If only they'd spent more time together before everything had fallen apart.

"It's like a burning pressure builds within. Imagine a fire stoked in your heart." His mother had smiled and poked him in the sternum. "Right there. Then, the world slows. You're mesmerized. And suddenly, something shifts. The tension eases. Your soul stretches until your very being is woven with that person. Your mate." His mother twirled away from him with her skirts fanning around her.

"But that's only the beginning, my little prince."

"What do you mean, Mother?"

His mother plopped down beside him on one of the ornate couches in the palace. "The thread starts thin and grows with time. A bond doesn't begin as unshakable as the one between your father and I."

"Thin? They can break?" Vas, merely fourteen at the time, had shaken his hair in front of his eyes to hide.

Her lips tilted downward. "They can break," she confirmed. "But struggling and growing together makes it worth it at the end. When you find your mate, don't let them go."

Vas didn't think he'd ever find his mate, but he'd nodded and said to his mother, "I won't ever let go."

And now? Could it be? He stared at Lana. Her smile. The way she spoke. So much like Anastasia, but not. How could Lana be his mate, when he still loved her sister? Yet, within himself, he felt the unmistakable glow of a thread stretching between them, tethering their souls together.

Lana made her choice — Liam — but Vas is keeping a secret. What will happen when Lana has to choose between the man she's loved all her life and the fae who is bound to her soul?

Find Out What Happens Next: Read More https://book s2read.com/Mosslight

Sneak Peek at Book 2: *Of Dreams and Mosslight*

She kept so many secrets, Lana thought as she looked down at her calloused hands.

These hands didn't belong to her. She clasped her fingers together, stretching the joints that still ached to move. This body had been asleep for decades, part of a spell her mother and Shiloh had worked to put up a wall, trapping the monsters terrorizing the fae. *Another of my mother's secrets.* A flash of anger rushed up, but Lana pushed it down, smothering it in the dark corners of her mind. *She had her reasons. She must have. Why else would she not tell me about my sister?*

At least Vas was here with her. Lana looked over at the quiet fae man, who sat staring at the city with a yearning expression. With his white hair, pointed ears, and stone gray skin, Vas was undeniably fae. His hair hung in messy curls and tangled at the base of his dark, ram-like horns, which jutted from his skull behind his ears. Despite his otherworldliness, he felt familiar to Lana. She decided it must be his eyes, bright green like Liam's, that made her feel so comfortable around him.

"So, where do you live in Haven?" Vas sat cross-legged on the ground, turning his head towards her with a curious tilt.

"I don't live there." Lana averted her gaze, picking at a loose thread on her trousers. "I'm not really from around here."

"But—" Vas cut himself off and turned around fully to look at her. His brows furrowed.

"It's complicated."

"Just like how it's complicated that you're related to Anastasia?"

"Yes," she said curtly. She wanted to trust him with the whole truth, but everything about the last day had made her wary. When had she ever been the type to follow strangers through portals or fight monsters?

Read More: https://books2read.com/Mosslight

Join the Faerie Friends Newsletter for updates on new releases, sales, and behind-the-scenes fun from A.J. Nora. When you sign up, you get a **FREE** ebook!

Twenty-five years ago, the Hollows rose from the shadows to torment all of Silvis. Alixandra Bludeg and Meredith Kaesy are knights sent to investigate strange rumors from the desert, but they are also fated mates.

Read *The Keeper of Light* to find out what happens between Alix and her mate, as well as how Vas and Anastasia first met! Read now for free:

https://dashboard.mailerlite.com/forms/1224485/140523304324695307/share

Thank you so much for reading! As an indie author, your support means everything to me. Without you, I wouldn't be able to continue writing the stories I love. If you'd like to help others fall in love with this story too, please consider leaving a review and telling your friends!

Here are some helpful links to show your support:

Review:

https://www.goodreads.com/book/show/229259124-the-court-of-dreams

Join the Newsletter:

https://dashboard.mailerlite.com/forms/1224485/140523304324695307/share

Follow me on social media: https://ajnorabooks.com/socials/

ABOUT THE AUTHOR

A.J. Nora is a queer (ace/pan-romantic) author from the deep south, who writes epic fantasy with romance. She loves swords and magic, fated mates, and faerie royalty. She became obsessed with faeries after reading the Fae Fever series when she was in high school. Ever since then, she's been writing down her daydreams, hoping to share them with the world.

If you'd like to come along on her indie author journey, follow A.J. on social media:

Join the Newsletter for book updates, sales, and exclusive stories:

https://dashboard.mailerlite.com/forms/1224485/14052 3304324695307/share

Facebook: https://m.facebook.com/61561948896462/

Instagram: https://www.instagram.com/ajnorabooks/

TikTok: https://www.tiktok.com/@ajnorabooks
Bluesky: https://bsky.app/profile/ajnorabooks.bsky.social
Tumblr: https://www.tumblr.com/ajnorabooks

ACKNOWLEDGEMENTS

This book (and the entire series) is well over ten years in the making. I would have never gotten this far without the love and support of my family and friends, especially my husband, Tyler, who has cheered me on (and read this book and many of my other creative endeavors). His love and belief in me made it possible for my dreams to succeed.

Then, there's my mom and grandparents, who have encouraged my creativity since I was a child, running around outside with the feral band of cats that lived in the woods behind my grandparents' house. I'm lucky to have such a supportive family and family-in-law.

Special thanks to one of my favorite people—Elyse, one of the first people to read the original draft of this book. There's all the readers who helped me work out the bumps along the road of this book. Thank you Cassie, Crissy, Erin, Ronni, Aunt LuAnne, Aunt Vicki, and Jackie.

Also, thank you to my editor Faith at the Atwater Group, who edited this manuscript, and Angela from Get-Covers who made the cover.

Last, but not least, I'd like to thank my writer friends in the Tally Writers discord group (especially Ashlea and Mikel, who I've chatted with often about bookish nonsense) and my critique group from TWA (Dr. Melanie Barton, Doris, Gwen, and Pat).

www.ingramcontent.com/pod-product-compliance
Lightning Source LLC
Chambersburg PA
CBHW031039310726
48969CB00007B/2046